HARRY

the

Wonder Cat

HARRY

the

Wonder Cat

THE LEGEND OF THE PINK DIAMOND

DENISE BRIXEY

LIFESTYLE
ENTREPRENEURS
PRESS
LAS VEGAS, NV

Publisher: Jesse Krieger
Write to Jesse@JesseKrieger.com if you are interested in publishing through Lifestyle Entrepreneurs Press.

Publications or foreign rights acquisitions of our catalogue books.
Learn More: www.LifestyleEntrepreneursPress.com

ISBN: 978-19-48787-80-2

Acknowledgment

This book has been a long time in the making. There are many who have contributed significantly in some way to *Harry the Wonder Cat*. First and foremost, I need to thank God, my Source, in making this dream come true. Next, a huge debt of gratitude goes to Mom and Dad who were my steadfast supporters when I doubted myself; to my friend Kym, who opened my eyes to the magic of cats; to Anne and Andrea for their gentle nudges when I needed them; to Musie for her exuberance from the very beginning; and of course to all of my cats who have enchanted me and provided their unconditional love. Thanks also to my editor Suze, who loves Harry almost as much as I do, and to Jesse and his gang at LE Press for their enthusiasm and guidance. There are many others I'd like to thank and although you may not be named, you know who you are. I have deep appreciation for all of you who helped bring Harry to life. May he now bring some magic into yours.

Dedication

This book is dedicated to all cats. You share your magic wherever you go, and life is much better for the people who are fortunate enough to have you caring for them.

Cast of Characters

NIKKI

HEATHER

GREG

ROBERT

SHERIFF

MARTHA

RHODA

TOM

ROXEY

MIRANDA

STU

HARRY

LITTLE BEA

OLLIE

DEWEY

Chapter 1

1815

"Harry."

Harry looked around and saw nothing but the ocean waves. As far as the eye could see...nothing. A light mist was in the morning air, and Harry could smell the scent of Spring. It had been a very cold Winter this year. Harry was grateful for his three layers of fur. Maine Coon cats were made for the cold, perfect for the freezing Maine weather, but he still preferred Springtime because the birds came out from hiding.

"Harry!"

Harry heard the voice again, but this time, it was more insistent. "Over here."

Harry turned to see another Maine Coon who he recognized as his grandfather. He was massive; twice as big as Harry's fifteen pounds. Harry's mother had told him that he came from a long line of huge cats and not to worry. Some day he will be big enough to be worthy of the name "Gentle Giant".

Harry heard the story about his grandfather, Sir Aslan, and how he received his honorary title. He had proven himself worthy by saving the princess from drowning. Of course, everyone knows that Maine Coons are exceptionally good swimmers. Anyway, the Cat King showed his gratitude by granting Sir Aslan his knighthood.

"Grand...I mean, Sir Aslan." Harry bowed in front of his grandfather.

"Get up, Harry. I come to you today, not as Sir Aslan, but as your grandfather." Sir Aslan was beaming. "You have been nominated for a knighthood and the Cat King is granting it."

Harry was visibly taken aback.

"B-b-but, Grandfather, I haven't done anything," Harry stuttered. "I haven't saved anyone like you did or..."

Sir Aslan held up his paw.

"Harry," Grandfather Aslan stopped him. "The Cat King sees real promise in you, as do I."

Harry humbly lowered his eyes.

"Now, hold on to me and I'll take us to the Cat Kingdom."

****

When Harry opened his eyes, he was in another world. He gazed around and saw that the sky overhead appeared to be painted in pastel pinks, purples and blues. He marveled at the beauty of this magical world. Harry turned and saw a rainbow shoot out from the ground and arc over the huge castle before him. The sky was full of glitter, and music could be heard—its origins seemed like everywhere and nowhere at once. This was the magical land that Harry had only heard about: the land of the Cat Kingdom.

"All of this is for you, Harry."

Sir Aslan smiled, patted Harry's head and advanced toward the gate house which protected the castle within. He looked over his shoulder at his bewildered grandson and harshly whispered to a stunned Harry, "Harry, come!"

Harry was shaken from his wonderment and ran to catch up with his grandfather. They slowly went through the gate house and Harry was humbled by the enormity of it. The cats who stood guard uncrossed their swords to let them in.

Once through the courtyard, they approached two more cats who were as still as statues until simultaneously bowing in reverence. "Sir Aslan."

Harry was proud of the respect the other cats had shown for his grandfather. *Maybe one day, it'll be me that they bow to!* The thought excited him.

Harry followed his grandfather into the Grand Hall that seemed to go on for miles. On the stone walls were tapestry after tapestry depicting the history of the most magnificent animals of all: cats. At each archway that they went through, two cat guards stood straight and tall, saluting Sir Aslan.

Finally they reached a red carpet. Grandfather stopped suddenly and Harry followed suit, looking up to see a magnificent crowned cat on a bejeweled throne. They waited for, what seemed to Harry like a century, and then the Cat King motioned Harry forward. His grandfather gave him a reassuring pat on the back and nodded.

Harry took a deep breath, willed his legs to move, held his head high and proceeded down the red carpet toward the King, as his grandfather looked on with pride. The King was wearing a royal blue robe and had a scepter encrusted with rubies, sapphires, emeralds and diamonds. Harry bowed down in front of the Cat King who then took his regal sword, tapped Harry on each shoulder, and said, "I hereby dub you Sir Harry."

Harry turned to see a tear fall from his grandfather's eyes. Sir Aslan quickly wiped it away.

"Sir Harry, along with your knighthood, magical powers are bestowed upon you. These powers will allow you to provide extraordinary care and comfort to generations of humans. I am assigning the Johnson family to you. Only the first-born Johnson of each generation shall know of your powers, and only when you deem fit."

A tall mirror was wheeled in and looking into it, Harry could see a family.

"The Johnsons will be under your care forever. You may have noticed that you're more aware of your surroundings. You need to follow your instincts, now more than ever. Whatever you do, do not let your powers be known to humans other than the first-born Johnson, or interfere with the deaths of the members of the family. In either case, you will be called out by me and stripped of your powers forever."

"What..." Harry interrupted and the King glowered at him.

After a time, the King continued, "You now have several powers, including eternal life, the ability to communicate with the dead, the ability to make yourself invisible, teleportation...and you will also be given the ability to read. "

The King noticed Harry's confused looked. "What's tel...tel...e... eport..."

"Teleportation—the ability to vanish from one place and appear at another," the King explained.

"Ohhh. How am I going to do all of these things?"

The Cat King pointed behind Harry.

"With that."

Harry turned around and couldn't believe his eyes. In front of him was a pink diamond. It sparkled and shone unlike any other stone that Harry had seen.

"How...?"

"Just pick it up."

Harry did as he was told. Suddenly, a warmth came over his whole body. He closed his eyes to savor the delicious feeling unlike any that he had felt in his whole life. When he opened his eyes and looked down at his paw, the diamond wasn't there. Harry was perplexed.

"What happened to it?"

The Cat King laughed. "It's all right, Harry. It's inside of you. You are The Pink Diamond. Use the magic that the diamond gives you to, not only care for the Johnson family, but teach them what is important in life. Now go on, Sir Aslan will deliver you to your first assignment.

Chapter 2

December 2018

Thursday, December 6th

Harry was on his special fence in the middle of town, which was known as "The Fence", where he met up with his gang almost every day. He loved this town after a fresh snowstorm. It was cool and the air was crisp. The sky was all pinks and purples, reminding him of the vivid sky over the Cat Kingdom. It was a beautiful evening in Harrot Reef.

Now Harry was ignoring the rest of the cats who were gathered there. He watched the hustle and bustle that Christmas brings to Harrot Reef. The snowstorm earlier today gave all of the kids ammunition for a major snowball fight in the town square. Next to the gazebo in the middle of the square, several men brought in a huge tree that Harry thought he would love to climb. Maybe tomorrow.

A siren sounded and Harry looked down the street. The firefighters had the old number 9 engine from back when the town was formed in 1815. *Back in the beginning. Back when I first began to live as The Pink Diamond and watch over the Johnson family.*

Across the alleyway was Abel's Groceries. It was a small store, but it seemed to have everything that this town needed. Down the street was the diner, a fine place to get a cheeseburger. Harry knew *that* from experience. For dessert, there's nothing like the bakery across the street.

Talk about fine dining...just down Kelly Hill, right across from the harbor, is The Twilight. They serve the best seafood in Maine. Their Lobster Thermidor is to die for!

Back on Main Street, next to the town square, is the Sheriff's Office. Mean old Sheriff O'Neil is the dirtiest, most underhanded man alive. He and his "Good ol' boy" pals are ruining this town with their political games and their taxes on the good citizens of the burg.

Harry didn't let their foolish games ruin his life. After all, he lived in the plushest home in town, with a fireplace in almost every room. When he came home from catting around, he could snuggle up with his charge, Lynn, next to a roaring fire. On those nights, Lynn would often read to him from his favorite author, Agatha Christie. Yes, life could not be better.

Little Bea was trying hard to get Harry's attention, but Harry's mind was miles away. Suddenly, his gray mane and tail fur fluffed out to its full extent. Harry felt a familiar tingle down his spine. His ears were filled with a screeching roar. Something was happening. Harry knew that whatever it was, was not good.

"Shh. Quiet!"

The gang all stopped what they were doing. Oh no. It was happening again. Harry's intuitive powers were at it once more. Harry cocked his head. His gang knew that he was intently listening for a cry of help.

Harry panicked, as he heard his charge's very soft voice. "Harry, where are you? I need you."

Little Bea stood still as a statue, holding her breath and looking wide eyed at her hero. Then, before they knew it, Harry was gone. Just vanished into thin air.

"I hate it when he does that."

"You're just jealous, Big Ron," Sox retorted.

Little Bea looked wistfully at the spot where, a second ago, Harry sat. She whispered, "I wish I could do that."

****

Harry appeared next to Lynn's body. He reached out his paw and put it gently on her chest. No movement. Her skin was already cold to the touch, even though the room was warmed by the roaring fire. Harry knew that he had lost Lynn. He knew also that, just like a mother with her children, he should not pick favorites. However, if anyone did ask him who was the most special of his charges, he would have to say Lynn.

Harry felt a lump in his throat and a tear escaped from his eye.

He whispered "Lynn...are you here?"

Suddenly a mist of white vapor came swirling from Lynn's lifeless body. Then the transparent image of Lynn was standing before him.

"Yes, Harry. I'm here, but just for a moment."

"What happened to you? How did you die?"

"I think I was poisoned. That's what I wanted to tell Nikki. I called her and told her to come early for Christmas...that something was terribly wrong. "

"*Poisoned?* By whom?"

Lynn shrugged her thin shoulders. That's just it...I don't know. All I know is that I've been so sick with what I thought was the flu or some kind of stomach virus that was oddly getting worse instead of better. The vomiting, etc. made me weak. And my gosh, the headaches! But I still attributed it all to being the flu. Until tonight. Tonight, the vomiting was worse than it had been before. The cramps were bad, Harry! Then I had a seizure and that was it."

Lynn noticed the tears forming in her loyal friend's eyes. "Harry, don't mourn me. I need you to keep it together so that you can do something for me."

"Anything."

"Nikki will be trying to find out who did this to me. I want you to look after her. She's going to be your new charge. Take care of her. Help her to cope with my passing. Oh, and don't forget to lead her to the letter."

"You know that you can count on me. I'll miss you, Lynn."

"I will be right here if I'm needed."

With that, the image faded into nothingness.

Harry looked around the room. Inspiration hit him. He trotted over to the table next to Lynn's chair where a book sat opened. It was "Murder on the Orient Express" by Agatha Christie. *No. That won't do.*

He reached a huge paw up to touch the book and vanished, only to reappear a microsecond later on the book shelf. He ran along the shelf that held the mysteries, reading the titles and finally stopping in front of one. He smiled to himself. *Yes!*

A few minutes later, he set the scene and settled himself down by Lynn, his charge.

****

"I want to thank you again, Heather."

"For what?"

"For coming with me to Harrot Reef. I know that you're busy writing that article for...what magazine was it?"

"Free Cult."

Heather felt Nikki shoot a disapproving look her way.

"Hey, it's a living." Heather shrugged. "It's only for one article. It's not like I work for them all the time." Heather paused for a moment. "Besides, we all can't be prolific authors like you. By the way, how is your latest coming?"

"It's not. I've hit a huge block. I have tried to get through it, but so far it's not happening."

"Maybe, once you see that your aunt's okay, you'll be able to get the juices flowing again," Heather suggested helpfully.

"Maybe."

Nikki had met Heather ten years ago when Nikki had moved to New York and bought a condo in the same building where Heather lived. Even though their social circles were different, they soon became fast friends. Nikki came from money and lots of it, and Heather came from a well-respected middle-class family. Heather had to work hard all of her life to get where she was today: a freelance writer who could write her own ticket.

Heather knew that when Nikki's mom and dad had gotten married, they had moved to California. Nikki was ten when they were in a car accident coming home from dinner one night. Nikki was sent to live with her Aunt Lynn in Harrot Reef, Maine. Heather often had asked Nikki why she moved from Maine to New York. Nikki's reply was always the same; she wanted to make it on her own.

She didn't want to go through life being handed everything on a silver platter. She wanted to be a writer and be recognized for her talent, not her family money. Aunt Lynn had started her at a very early age on Agatha Christie's classics. Murder on the Orient Express and Death on the Nile were her favorites. From that age on, all she wanted to do was to write mysteries like Agatha. Now she is working on the fourth book in her own series that she started eighteen months ago.

Nikki's thoughts turned to why she was speeding down the freeway. Aunt Lynn had called her last night, telling her that she'd better come to Harrot Reef right away. She was sick and she needed Nikki to be there. Aunt Lynn had said that something strange was going on. When Nikki asked what, Aunt Lynn just whispered that she couldn't talk about it over the phone. She told her just to come as soon as possible.

Heather had insisted on coming with Nikki, and Nikki was glad that she did. There was no telling what awaited her in Harrot Reef. She might need Heather's assistance with Aunt Lynn.

As they approached the manor house, Nikki took a moment to take it all in. The three-story Victorian had always been magnificent, the grandest house in town. It was pastel yellow with a clean white gingerbread trim. It had several peaks and, at the very top, a widow's walk, which was used by several Johnson women throughout the years, waiting for their men to return from the sea. Aunt Lynn had refurbished the house, enlarging some of the bedrooms upstairs by knocking down walls, making two rooms into one. She updated the kitchen and the bathrooms, but kept the atmosphere of days gone by in the rest of the manor house.

The third level was a mystery to all of the kids in the family. They were never allowed to go beyond the second floor, so the children would tell stories of ghosts and other monsters who lived in the attic. Nikki had always felt that it possessed something magical when she was a child. Even now, as an adult, the house still held mysteries for her.

As Nikki parked the car, Heather looked around at the snow, glistening under the Christmas lights that enveloped the manor and transformed it to a castle from a fairytale.

"It's so beautiful now. Much different from the last time I was here last Summer. I can see why you come up here for Christmas every year."

Nikki smiled at her friend and tried not to show how anxious she was to get in to see her aunt.

"Aunt Lynn. We're here." Nikki and Heather put their heavy suitcases down in the front hall. "Aunt Lynn. Where are you?"

A loud howling sound was the only answer. Nikki looked at her friend. The sound was coming from the library.

Nikki ran down the long hallway, and stopped dead in her tracks when she saw what had happened in the room. There usually was a fire that would give off a warm glow, but now it was cold. The fire had died out. She saw her aunt lying in a heap on the hearth and Harry, the Johnson's huge gray and black Maine Coon sitting over her and making the most pitiful sound that Nikki had ever heard.

"Aunt Lynn?"

Heather walked past Nikki and knelt beside the body. Immediately, she smelled a slight garlicky scent emitting from Lynn's mouth. From extensive research done for an article she previously wrote on poisons, the possibility of arsenic poisoning popped into her head. She took Lynn's pulse, looked up at her friend and shook her head.

"Oh, no!" Nikki stared at her Aunt Lynn; dead and sprawled out right in front of her. She knelt beside her aunt and cradled her head.

Heather took in her surroundings. In the center of the far wall, was a fireplace with a black marble mantle, polished to a sheen. On either side of it were built-in bookcases filled with books of all genres. The overstuffed chairs in front of the fireplace were covered with deep, green silk brocade that matched the silk on the walls. A roll top desk looked out over the expanse of snow and beyond to the sea. Portraits of Johnsons from decades past hung from heavy gold chains.

It was obvious that Lynn had been sitting in front of the fireplace, as there was an open book on the antique side table. Heather grabbed a tissue from the box on the table and flipped the book closed. The title was "The Mysterious Affair at Styles". Her eye caught something on the floor next to the chair.

Heather bent down and saw a teacup in pieces on the oriental carpet. Right in front of the table was a dark spot next to the broken cup. Being careful not to touch it, Heather hesitantly extended her arm out and felt dampness. She held her long red hair back, and bent to smell spot. Tea. Not a normal blend, but a mix of herbs and something else. Something she couldn't quite put her finger on. Was it garlic?

Heather rocked back off of her knees and onto her feet and caught sight of a slip of paper folded in half in amongst the Christmas cards on the mantle. If she wasn't looking for something out of the ordinary, Heather wouldn't have noticed it. It might have been mistaken for another yuletide message. She unfolded and read it. Heather quickly stuffed in her back pocket of her jeans.

Heather guided Nikki out of the room. "Let's go into the living room. I'll call the sheriff from there." Heather put her arm around her friend and led her away from that horrible sight. She helped Nikki to sit down and walked across the room where the telephone was and got the number to the Sheriff's Office.

"We need some help at the Harrot Reef Manor now! Lynn Johnson is dead." Heather was quiet for a moment and then, "I don't know. She was just on the library floor when her niece and I came in." Again, someone asked her a question. "No. Nikki and I had come up here from New York. When we got here, she was dead. Now, can you get over here, please?" She slammed down the phone. Heather was running out of patience.

Whoever it was who said that redheads have a short temper, had Heather in mind.

Turning her attention to Nikki, "I'll get you some water."

Heather disappeared into the kitchen. Within a few seconds she was standing next to Nikki, holding a glass out to her.

"Here. Drink this. "

Nikki accepted the glass. Heather turned and lit the fire, and thought about the piece of notepaper she had found on the mantle in the other room. She had tucked it safely in her jeans pocket and now, she retrieved it. It had only one word on it:

'Goodbye.'

"What's that, Heather?"

Heather slowly looked up at Nikki. She had a decision to make. Should she tell her that her aunt left a note and obviously committed suicide right now, while she was so upset, or should she wait until things settled a bit?

Too late, Nikki made her decision for her when she stood and grabbed the note away from Heather. Nikki read it and let go a strangled gasp.

Shaking her head, "No! Aunt Lynn would not do this! Someone else must have made her write this."

"So, you're saying that somebody...murdered her? That's jumping to conclusions, Nikki. Besides, your aunt was loved by everyone, and you know it."

"Heather, you've known her for years. Do you honestly think that she could kill herself? Besides, how did she do it? Did you see anything that she could have done it with? She didn't have anything, like sleeping pills, in the house. Aunt Lynn didn't believe in traditional medicine."

"She could have put something in the tea." Heather thought of the garlicky smell.

"Like what? As I said, Aunt Lynn only took natural remedies. Essential oils, herbs and teas."

"Okay. So, maybe she knew that she was going to die, and at the last minute..."

"What? She wrote a note? I doubt that very seriously. No, Heather. It has to be murder."

Nikki's mind went to all of the things that she did with her aunt. Aunt Lynn was always fun. She took her shopping, after which, she would take her out to lunch at The Twilight Tavern, which was a block away from the harbor. There was a wall of glass windows on the harbor side of the restaurant. It was there that Nikki would always sit and watch the boats sailing just outside the harbor. The boardwalk, which ran alongside the harbor, was packed on a bright Summer's day.

It was thoughts of these trips that Heather interrupted. "The deputy said that they would be here in about a half an hour. Why don't you lie down until then?"

Nikki swung her feet around to lie down. She sighed. How could anybody do this to Aunt Lynn? She never hurt anyone. She was well liked in the town. Well, except for Sheriff Grady O'Neil, but he has always had it out for the Johnsons, ever since Dad "stole" Mom's heart from him.

"Do you want anything? A cup of cocoa, anything?"

Nikki just lay there in a daze. Heather sat down on the other side of the room and watched her friend as she continued to gaze at the fire. Tears were trickling down Nikki's face. Heather felt helpless. She wanted to make it all go away, to turn back time.

Even the knock that sounded at the door didn't move Nikki's gaze from the fire. Heather stood and opened the door. She didn't notice Harry standing behind the fern in the hall.

"Okay. What's the matter, little lady?"

Heather immediately felt her hackles rise. He was condescending and it was obvious that he thought women couldn't think or do for themselves. He was short and rotund. He had beady little eyes that were nondescript in color and was bald, with the exception of a salt and pepper ring of short hair that encircled his overly large head. He had, what looked to be, a permanent scowl on his face. It was only when he pushed past her, she smelled the sickening stench of stale cigar.

Now, the deputy behind him was quite a different story. One look in his kind eyes, and Heather relaxed. He was about her age, had brown hair cut short and had a scruffy beard that looked good on his handsome face. His uniform fit nicely too. He stood there until Heather opened the door wider and motioned him in.

He turned to her. "Good evening, miss. I'm very sorry for your loss." He bowed his head slightly.

"Thank you. Nikki is in here, deputy, and Lynn is down the hall, in the library."

The sheriff was already in the living room, looming over Nikki, and Heather thought, just for a minute, he was going to accuse her of killing her own aunt.

He just smirked and shook his massive head. "Now don't get hysterical, little lady. We will take care of this for you. In the meanwhile, questions have to be answered...truthfully."

Heather had just about enough of this condescending, self-righteous jerk. Nikki had told her the history between her father and him, but that was no reason for this kind of treatment. Nikki was so fragile at this point, Heather was afraid that her friend would crumble right before their very eyes.

Then the questions came as fast as lightning.

"Where were you today? Why did you come here? Do you have any proof that you were not here when she died?"

"Okay. That's it. Are you accusing Nikki of murdering her aunt?"

"Of course not, little lady. These are just questions that I have to ask."

Next to Heather, Nikki quietly sobbed.

"Look. Is there any way that these questions can wait until tomorrow? As you can see, she is in no shape to answer anything."

O'Neil scowled at Heather and she knew that he didn't like her. Well, that was okay. She didn't like him either. He shook his head in disgust. When he saw the Medical Examiner walk through the front door, he turned to leave the room.

"Holloway, handle this," he commanded. He followed the coroner into the library.

"Okay, Grady," the coroner said without looking up. "Smell that garlicky odor?"

O'Neil nodded.

"Based on that and the chronic symptoms she's been having... well, those *could* be signs of arsenic poisoning."

"*Arsenic?*" A smile crept across O'Neil's face. He removed the toothpick from his mouth. "So...then we' talking *murder?*"

O'Neil has been waiting over 40 years to catch a Johnson doing something wrong.

"Could this be murder?" O'Neil repeated, perhaps a little too excitedly. "And if it is, could the girl...could Nikki have done it?"

"Whoa! I said it *could* be arsenic. We can't tell until the toxicology report comes back. As far as Nikki killing Lynn...I don't know. All I can tell you is that based on what I'm seeing here, Lynn's been dead since between 12 noon and three...no more than four p.m. at the latest. It would depend on if Nikki was here at that time."

Sitting in the corner listening, was Harry. He was using his power of invisibility to hide so that he could overhear what was going on without bringing attention to himself. He had heard the sheriff and it didn't take a rocket scientist to know what his plan was. *We'll just see about that!* Harry popped out of the library and into the living room, where he could watch a different drama unfold.

Deputy Holloway, who was perched on the velvet chair next to the fireplace, said in his deep voice, "Can you get her a cup of tea or something?"

"She hates tea," Heather answered.

When he gave her a pained look, she quickly covered her tracks. "I'll see what there is in the kitchen."

Heather came in, moments later with a cup of steamy, hot cocoa. "Would you like something, deputy?"

He raised his hand and shook his head no. He waited until Nikki took a few sips of her drink.

"Now," he said in a low voice that was like velvet. It probably came in useful when he was questioning a woman, as it was so soothing and reassuring. "Can you answer some of those questions?"

Nikki couldn't seem to find her voice.

"Take your time. How about let's start simple. What time did you find your aunt?"

"Just after 5:00 p.m." Nikki's voice was barely a whisper.

"Good. Now, were you driving from New York, or did you travel another way?"

"Yes, by car."

"Did you stop along the way?"

Nikki looked confused.

"Yes, we did," Heather chimed in. "Rick's Place."

He looked back up to Heather. "What is "Rick's Place"? A restaurant? A bar? What?"

"It's a coffee shop just on the other side of the Maine border," Nikki answered.

"And what time did you get there?" the deputy asked Nikki.

"I don't know. We had lunch there, so I guess it was sometime in the early afternoon."

"How long were you there? Approximately."

"I don't know. We were in a hurry to get here. We got take-out to eat in the car, so about 15 to 20 minutes." Nikki looked helplessly at Heather.

Harry knew that Nikki needed his support, so he leapt on her lap, and attempted to soothe her nerves with his purring. Nikki looked down at him and began to pet him.

"You wouldn't have a receipt, would you?" the deputy asked softly.

Nikki looked at Heather who shrugged and said, "I know I paid for it on my credit card, but I don't know where the receipt got to, unless you picked it up."

"I can't remember." Nikki turned back to the deputy. "Does that matter?"

"It would make things a lot easier. A receipt would have the date and time stamped on it, so it would help to establish where you both were at the time of death. Okay. Let's see." He looked at his notes. "You came to spend Christmas with Lynn, right?"

"Yes. Well, we were supposed to come up six days before Christmas, but Aunt Lynn called last night and asked us to come as soon as possible instead. She said it was urgent."

The deputy was writing in his notepad, when the sheriff came in. Heather and Nikki looked up to see the sheriff pick up the note that Heather had left on the table.

"What is this?"

The deputy stood and walked toward him. He took the note from O'Neil's hand, read it, then gave it to Heather.

"Yeah. I forgot to tell you. That was on the mantle when we found Lynn," Heather explained.

"Well? Do you think that it would have been important? Someone probably forced her to write this." O'Neil looked pointedly at Nikki. "Or wrote it themself."

Deputy Holloway jumped to Nikki's defense. "It could be a plain and simple suicide."

Nikki finally found her voice. "No! Aunt Lynn would not commit suicide." She turned to O'Neil. "You knew her, sheriff. She loved her life too much to throw it away."

"Then what do you think happened? Somebody broke in to kill her? Everything is locked up tight as a drum. She was alone, unless you were here earlier than you said. In which case, you have a lot of questions to answer." O'Neil sneered.

Nikki's eyes widened and her mouth opened, but no sound came out.

Heather glanced at her, and came to her rescue. "When was the time of death?"

"The coroner's initial exam indicates that time of death was between noon and 3 p.m., 4 at the latest."

"Sheriff, we were not here until after 5 p.m."

"Well, we'll see. I want you both to come into the station first thing in the morning to answer more questions."

The sheriff nodded to the deputy and said in his baritone voice, "C'mon Holloway," before he spun around and walked out the door.

The deputy turned and gave an apologetic smile. "Take care of her," he said to Heather. "Come in anytime tomorrow morning to finish up."

He bowed his head slightly and left the house.

Heather turned to see Nikki looking absolutely spent, as if she couldn't take another minute of this nightmare.

"Hey, Nikki. Why don't you go up and try to get some sleep."

Nikki nodded in response and slowly climbed the stairs.

Heather went into the kitchen to clean up the cup and pot from Nikki's cocoa. She wiped down the counter and something caught her eye. There, next to the stove, was a small tin container. She picked it up and read the label. 'Pu-erh Tea'.

"Strange kind of tea. Oh well, Nikki said that Lynn drank some unusual teas. "

Heather thought nothing more about it as she put it in the cupboard along with all of the other tea, before making her own way up to bed.

Chapter 3

Friday, December 7th

Nikki awoke confused. She asked herself what day it was—Friday. She looked around and then realized that she was at Aunt Lynn's. Now the memories came flooding back. Aunt Lynn lying dead on the floor. The sheriff all but accusing Nikki of killing her own aunt. Her stomach clenched tight with fear. What if he actually put her in jail? She could be in prison for the rest of her life for something she didn't do. It happened all of the time. Considering the amount of hate that O'Neil had for Nikki's family, she wouldn't be surprised if he arrested her on trumped up charges.

Nikki grabbed her fleece robe and tucked her freezing feet into her fur lined slippers, and walked downstairs. She found that Heather was frying bacon and had eggs and bread ready to go after it was done. The room smelled of cherry chocolate coffee and bacon, and in spite of herself, she realized that she was hungry...very hungry.

"You didn't have to go to all this trouble. I would have been fine with coffee," said Nikki.

"Nonsense. We need to eat. We haven't had a bite since lunch yesterday." Heather poured some coffee for her, and Nikki accepted it gratefully.

Nikki smelled the rich aroma and closed her eyes. She was in heaven. There was nothing she liked better than to wake up to a really good cup of coffee...except maybe the smell of bacon frying.

After taking the first sip of her coffee, she offered to help with the breakfast. "Well, the bacon is not quite done, so we have to hold off on the eggs, but you can pop some bread in to make toast."

Nikki immediately set to her task.

Heather looked at her friend. She was worried about her. There were dark circles under her eyes, indicating a lack of sleep. "Did you get any rest last night?"

"Not really. I laid in bed wondering what happened. How could Aunt Lynn just keel over and die like that?"

"Did she have any medical problems?"

Nikki shook her head.

"No heart problems?" Heather asked.

"No, she was healthy. She ran five miles and then swam like a fish in the town's indoor pool every single day. She would even fly down to Boston and run the marathon every year. She played tennis, racquetball and handball."

"So, she was an athlete?"

"Well, I don't know if you would call her an athlete, but she was very active. She was also very happy, so I know it wasn't suicide. It was murder. Out and out murder! There wasn't a wound that I could see, so it had to be something she ate or drank."

An idea came to Heather. Taking the tea container from the cabinet, she handed it to Nikki. "I found this on the table last night."

"Pu-erh tea?" Nikki asked.

"Yeah. I've heard of it but forgot exactly where," Heather said, as she put the container back in its place.

"My aunt did drink the strangest imported tea ever. She drank this one to control her blood pressure. In fact, I usually brought her a box whenever I came up, but I couldn't find it the last couple of times before I visited. I guess she got that box from somewhere around here." Nikki hesitated. "Hey, I recall hearing that this tea contains a small amount of arsenic. Could that be what killed her? No, she is way too careful to drink too much of it," Nikki answered her own question.

Heather hated what she was thinking. Nikki didn't have it in her to harm a fly, let alone kill her own aunt. Still, she did admit to bringing Lynn the tea when she came to visit.

"Nikki. Does the sheriff know that? I mean about the arsenic and that you usually buy her the tea?"

"I don't think so. At least not yet. I'm not sure if I should tell him or not."

Heather looked at Nikki doubtful. "Okay. Say it had extra arsenic in it, how did it get in the box?"

"No idea. As far as I know she only had lots of friends."

And at least one enemy, Heather thought. Nikki says that she didn't care about the family money, but Heather knew for a fact that she was beginning to have second thoughts about living in New York. Heather knew that Nikki loved it here, and she hated the big city life, no matter how much she denied it. Nikki would probably inherit the Harrot Manor, as she was the last remaining Johnson in her family. Her mom and dad died years ago, and she had no siblings. Aunt Lynn was her father's sister and had never married or had children, so the family home, along with all the money that came with it, would go to Nikki. She would be set for life. Heather was torn from her thoughts.

"One of them could have sneaked it in."

"Wouldn't she catch them?" Heather was skeptical.

"Not necessarily. Aunt Lynn had parties all the time. All anyone would have to do is wait until they were alone in the kitchen and put the poison in the box. "

"Okay. What have we got? She was found on the library floor with "The Mysterious Affair at Styles" on the table next to her chair. Now, what was that one about?" Heather wanted to know.

"It was by Agatha Christie about this woman who was poisoned and it was thought that the tea cup which was found ground to dust on the floor, contained the poison. Do you think that was a clue? Maybe Aunt Lynn was trying to tell us that she *was* poisoned." Nikki's eyes were glistening with tears.

"Could be. At this point, we can't discount anything. I found a tea cup, but ours was broken, not ground into the carpet."

"Okay, granted; but who would have hated my aunt so much that they would kill her? Everybody in this town loved her. She did a lot of good. She gave the money for a new library. She bought a new engine for the fire department, to say nothing about what she did for the city hall. It was falling down before she had it rebuilt from the foundation up."

Heather chased from her head the thoughts about Nikki killing Lynn for the money. Instead, she chastised herself. *You should be ashamed of yourself. After all that Nikki has done for you, how could you think she was capable of doing something as despicable as murdering someone?*

"Breakfast is ready."

"When we finish with the sheriff, why don't we have lunch at Martha's?" Nikki suggested.

"Sounds like a plan to me. We can stop at the bakery and get some goodies?"

Nikki nodded her head, with no enthusiasm.

After breakfast, Heather decided that keeping Nikki moving would probably prevent her from thinking too much about what was going on. Doing the daily chores may keep her mind on what she is doing instead of dwelling on the current reality.

"Come on, slowpoke," Heather said from the top of the stairs.

Nikki just gave her a pained look. "I don't feel like moving fast today."

"You'll feel better after a shower."

"I doubt it" and with that said Nikki turned to go into her room.

After her shower, Nikki donned some long underwear, a pair of jeans and a pale blue cable knit sweater. She slipped her feet into thick, woolen socks and pulled on fur-lined boots. She stood in front of the full length mirror and saw the bags under her swollen blue eyes. She was going to ignore them and just dry her long blond hair, but she decided that she might feel better if she made herself up a bit. She expertly applied mascara and a little blush and finished it off with a pale pink lipstick. She examined the results and saw that she looked no better than before.

"What a waste of time that was," Nikki said to her reflection.

When Nikki came down the stairs, she saw Harry curled up by the fire. He was beautiful...and big. Huge, in fact. His long fur was glistening in the light from the fire. His eyes were a golden color, and held the mysteries of all of the ages. His square face was that of a regal king and his large ears perked up as Nikki walked into the room.

Harry allowed Nikki to pick him up and bury her face in his wild mane.

"I was wondering where you were, Harry. You must be hungry."

Nikki eased the cat down to the floor, and started toward the kitchen, with Harry following closely behind. Heather was pouring two cups of coffee, when Nikki and Harry came in.

"Well, hello Harry."

"He's hungry," Nikki said.

The cat walked straight to a cupboard a sat in front of it.

Heather giggled. "Look! He seems to know where it is."

"Yeah, that cupboard is called The Magic Cupboard because when I was young, I thought that since Harry seemed to know where to go for his goodies, it was magic. I started calling it the Magic Cupboard and it stuck."

Harry gazed at Heather. "Trill."

"I'll never get used to that sound!"

Nikki reached down to pet him. "He's talking to you."

"I know, but I've only heard Harry "talk" like that."

"You've never been around Maine Coons then. Instead of meowing, Maine Coons trill most of the time."

Nikki opened the cupboard and found a bag of dry food, eight cans of unopened wet food and two bags of cat treats. When Harry put his paw on one of the bags of treats, both of the women broke into laughter. Nikki stooped down and retrieved the bag from the shelf. As soon as she opened it, he stuck his nose in, followed by his paw to steady it.

Nikki smiled as the cat got a treat out with his big paw. She scooped some dry food into his dish and gave him some fresh water. Harry lunged at the dish and began to gobble the food without even taking the time to chew. Nikki stood in front of him for a moment with her arms crossed. She shook her head and couldn't help but smile.

Heather picked up Nikki's purse and handed it to her.

"We might just as well get this over with."

Nikki sighed, snatched her purse away from her friend, and started for the door.

****

When they arrived at the Sheriff's Office, Nikki stopped cold.

Even though it was a relatively new building, when Aunt Lynn had agreed to give the county the money to rebuild, she had one stipulation: that it wouldn't lose its charm. It must fit in with the rest of the town. As a result, the building was made from stone and mortar. Wide curved stairs that stretched the length of the building led to a door with the words "Harrot Reef Sheriff's Office" in gold letters etched on it .

"You have to do this sooner or later, so let's do it now. It's not like you're going in there alone. I'll be with you all the way," Heather said in a soothing tone.

Heather gave her a little nudge to the door. Once inside, Nikki hung back while Heather stepped up to the reception counter. The duty officer, Officer Ryan, was busy with paperwork, although in a town this size there can't be too much going on.

Heather stood there waiting for him to look up. When he didn't, she cleared her throat. Still nothing. She tried a new tactic, tapping her well manicured bright red nails on the desk. Still no response.

"Excuse me," Heather said in the nicest tone possible under the circumstances. She wasn't used to getting ignored by anyone, especially men.

When he finally looked up, his body exuded annoyance. "Yeah?"

Well, two can play this game, Heather thought. "Right. Well, we," she gently pulled Nikki up next to her, "are supposed to come in to be interviewed. See, my friend…"

"Yeah, right." The officer let go a heavy sigh, and heaved himself off his stool. Then he disappeared into the back for a few minutes, and came back, sat on his stool and continued with his paperwork.

Before she could say what she was really thinking, Heather saw Deputy Holloway come through the door marked 'Personnel Only'.

With a smile on his face, the deputy said, "Good morning, ladies. Come on in."

It was a tiny room with four desks, but only three had name plates on them. The biggest desk belonged to, of course, the sheriff. As expected, it fitted his personality to a tee. It was covered with empty file folders and papers strewn across the desk that presumably once had been in order, but now they were in such a state that Heather could not tell which paper belonged in which folder. A full ashtray had taken its place among the mess. Heather spied the cigar, probably from the night before.

The deputy led them past the filthy mess and to his own desk. In contrast to the larger desk, the deputy's was as neat as a pin. Folders were stacked in organized piles on the left side of the otherwise spotless desk.

He offered each of them a chair. Nikki, nervous as a cat, looked over at her friend. Heather appeared perfectly calm, even a little put out.

The deputy cleared his throat. "Now I don't want you to be scared, Nikki. A lot of these are the same questions that I asked you last night. They are just for our files."

Nikki slowly nodded her head keeping her eyes on her hands in her lap.

"About when did you come into Harrot Reef last night?"

Heather started to answer but the deputy raised his hand to silence her. "I'd like to hear it from you, Nikki."

"I guess just before 5 o'clock, like we told you last night."

"Okay. So, you came in the house, and then what?"

"I called out for Aunt Lynn, but she didn't answer, but I heard Harry howling."

"Harry?" The deputy had a confused look.

"My aunt's cat."

"Oh, okay. And then what?"

"I knew something was wrong so I followed Harry's howling which took me into the library."

Holloway stopped writing in his pad. He looked up at Nikki and asked, "So, you went straight to the library?"

"Yes. I followed Harry's howling."

A look of confusion flashed on the deputy's face. "And then you saw your aunt?"

Heather cut in. "I checked for her pulse and found none. Then we went into the other room and I called you guys."

"So, then you just waited for us to come?"

"Yes." Heather thought that was obvious.

"What about the note?" queries the deputy.

"What about it?" Heather asked.

"When did you notice it?"

"Right after I checked her pulse."

Suddenly, the sheriff burst in the room and began to bellow at the deputy. "What are you doing? Are you questioning them?"

O'Neil stomped over to them and towered over Holloway. "You should know by now that we do not question more than one suspect at a time!" He grabbed Heather's arm and pulled her up.

Heather resisted, pulled her arm back, and exclaimed, *"Excuse me? We* are suspects? Why?"

"Because you were there; because you were the first one on the scene; and because you found her," snapped the sheriff.

"Hey Grady...I mean, sheriff," Holloway started and stopped as soon as the sheriff interrupted.

"You claim to be a professional. If you were, you'd realize that these ladies are our number one suspects."

O'Neil grabbed Heather again and roughly led her to a windowless room that reminded Heather of a cell. It had a gray metal table that was dented from years of suspects pounding their fists on it, trying to make their point. The sheriff slammed the door shut and Heather found herself locked away with the most loathsome man she had ever met.

Out at the deputy's desk, Nikki was trying her best not to break down. She answered Holloway's questions in a daze, until he questioned her about the relationship that she had with her aunt.

Nikki's eyes came alive with anger. "Deputy, my aunt was the only family I had left! Of course, our bond was like mother and daughter. She raised me since the age of five after my parents were killed in a car accident. I don't know what I am going to do without her. Does that answer your question?"

"Yes." Holloway hesitated. "Nikki, listen. I have to ask these questions. They are the standard questions that we ask everybody. I'm really sorry, but it's my job."

Nikki just nodded her head. The questioning went on for what seemed like hours and finally the girls were able to leave.

The last thing that they heard as they were going through the door was the sheriff booming, "Don't leave town!"

****

As they entered the only diner in town, Nikki looked around and, once again, marveled at the way that nothing had changed in Martha's Hangout since her high school days, over ten years ago. The floor was the same black and white checkered design. On the walls were several nostalgic pictures and records of old-fashioned rock 'n roll stars like Buddy Holly, Elvis, Fats Domino and Sam Cooke. The booths were still of bright red vinyl, with several pieces of silver tape where splits in the cloth had been haphazardly covered. Each of the intimate tables still had a miniature jukebox and the obligatory condiments and metal napkin holders with sticky fingerprints from kids.

The square white tables in the middle of the room were off-white now and had a lot more stains on them than before. The straight back chairs still were the most uncomfortable chairs that Nikki had ever sat on.

There were six metal, backless stools, the kind with black vinyl on top, pulled up to the same old counter. It still was an awful pale blue color with white specks.

The only difference was the fake pink and silver Christmas tree with white frosted bulbs hanging on the sparse branches, standing in the corner. It must have been at least ten years old, and was lit from behind by a spotlight with a multicolor screen that rotated, changing the color of the tree.

Martha, the owner of the diner, stood behind the counter, talking animatedly to the only customer in the place. She had the energy and the exuberance of an 18 year old. All a person had to do was to look at Martha, with her twinkling blue-green eyes and her deep dimples, and they would realize at once that this was a woman who loved life.

Ten years ago when her husband Reggie was lost at sea and presumed dead, life as she knew it was gone. She was left to raise their nine year old daughter by herself. Her outlook changed when Martha took all of their savings and bought The Coffee Cup Cafe. She brought new life into this place. Immediately, it became *the* hangout for the high school kids. That was when she changed the diner's name to Martha's Hangout.

Nikki caught Martha's eye and raised her hand in a slight wave. Martha nodded her way, refilled the woman's cup of coffee and came up to Nikki and hugged her.

"Nikki, it is so good to see you! I heard you were in town. I'm so sorry about your aunt."

"How did you...? Oh, don't tell me. I keep forgetting that this is not New York. Bad news travels like wildfire here."

Martha nodded. "Yeah, I'm afraid so."

"It's really good to be back and see all of my old friends, but it's not going to be the same without Aunt Lynn."

"We all know that she wasn't feeling well for a month before she passed," Martha said.

"Well, I knew that she wasn't feeling well for the last few weeks, but when she asked me to come early, I knew it had to be more than just a flu, but she never said anything major was going on. Did she see a doctor at least?"

"Yes. You know Dr. Sweeney?

"Yeah. What did he think it was?" Nikki didn't approve of Dr. Sweeney, but her aunt was too stubborn to see that he was a quack.

"He didn't know. When she began to get worse last week, Dr. Sweeney sent a nurse named Robert to take care of her during the daytime. He helped her with her daily routines, cooking, and even did light housekeeping. Dr. Sweeney was still doing tests when she..." Martha averted her eyes.

"Why didn't she tell me before now? We'd always tell each other everything," Nikki said.

Martha patted Nikki on her shoulder. "She didn't want to worry you. She honestly felt it was nothing but a case of the flu and that she would get over it by Christmas."

"So, maybe I'll speak to Robert first and then go and see Dr. Sweeney, since the nurse would probably know more of how Aunt Lynn was behaving at the end," Nikki said.

"He is out of town. He left Monday, but I think he's coming back in a few days."

"If she was so sick, why did he go off and leave her?"

"Rhoda was going to check on her a few times a day," Martha answered.

"You are kidding. Aunt Lynn should have had a professional with her at all times, not her neighbor. What could Rhoda do? Why wasn't I called? I could have been here in a few hours."

Martha laid her hand on Nikki's. "I know, dear, but as I said before, your aunt didn't want a fuss. She thought that it was just a bad case of flu. For that matter, so did everyone else. You know, it's going around. Why, I heard the Sadie Robinson has been laid up for a week with it, and..."

Nikki interrupted, "Thanks, Martha."

Heather smiled at Martha, who looked at her questionably. "So who's this?" Martha asked.

"You remember Heather."

"Oh, of course I do. I'm sorry I didn't recognize you all bundled up."

Heather said, "That's okay Martha. It's good to see you again."

Martha smiled. "As you can see, we aren't really busy today, so take your pick of tables."

Nikki looked around. She looked at Martha with a concerned look in her eye.

"Martha are you...is the diner in trouble?"

Martha answered fast. "Oh, no. We're fine, it's just slow right now because of the snow. It'll get busy again when school starts."

Martha picked up two menus from the stack near the cash register.

Nikki and Heather took a seat at a booth and opened the menus.

"I think I'll have..." Nikki started.

"Cheeseburger and fries and a chocolate shake," Martha said as she wrote it down on her pad.

"How'd you know?"

"You've only been ordering the same thing since you started coming here."

They all laughed. Heather ordered the same.

When Martha was gone, they leaned across the table and started talking in low voices about Sheriff O'Neil.

"So you've had to deal with that freak for all of your life?"

Martha came with their milkshakes and told them, "Cheeseburgers up soon".

Nikki took a long pull at her straw and savored the sweet liquid as it cooled her throat. "Yep. I don't know how my father ever got along with him. That is to say, before the feud."

"You never told me about a feud."

"It really was just a silly kid thing. Back when they were in high school...it must be forty years ago now. Dad and O'Neil competed for everything from the quarterback position, to the girls they were dating. When it came to my mother, O'Neil thought he had first dibs. My mother only had eyes for my father, and could care less about O'Neil. This created a hatred that lasted until Dad died."

"So, that's all it is. Why does O'Neil take it out on you, though? You had nothing to do with it."

"I know. O'Neil wants to control everyone in this town, and it really irks him that Dad got the best of him. He's been trying to get back at the Johnsons since. Now that Aunt Lynn had died, I guess I'm the only Johnson left to control."

When their cheeseburgers and fries came, they dug into them like they hadn't eaten in days. Heather looked around at the restaurant. "I've liked this place from the first time you brought me here. It has a sort of homey feeling."

Heather knew that Nikki was really upset about what had happened in the sheriff's department, so she tried to get her to talk about something else.

"Was your family home named for the town, Harrot Reef, or vice versa?"

"The town was named after the manor."

"How did that happen?" Heather prodded.

"It's a long boring story. You sure you want to hear it?"

Heather nodded her head.

"In 1815, four generations ago, my great-great grandfather on my father's side came from England to settle down. He chose to build the manor on the hill overlooking the ocean and he called it Harrot Reef Manor. I don't know why, so don't ask me."

Heather smiled. She held up her hands in surrender. "I wasn't going to."

"The house was a lot smaller than it is today."

"They expanded it?"

"Yeah, but get this...the house had burned not once, not twice but *three* times since it was first built. Can you believe it?"

Heather's eyes widened. "That is so bizarre!"

"Every time they rebuilt it, they added onto it so that now it is what you see today. Anyway, my family was the first to settle in this area and when others came to live, they formed a township and they called it Harrot Reef after the Johnson family home."

"Really? That's so cool!"

"Yeah, I guess it is. I never thought of it like that," Nikki said between fries. Her eyes glazed over, as she thought about the days of her childhood. "Did I ever tell you about the legend?"

"No, what legend?" Heather leaned forward, wanting to catch every word.

"Well, when I was just a kid, I can remember hearing other family members talk about my crazy great-Uncle Frank who apparently told a story about winning a diamond in a high stakes poker game. That night, my uncle almost lost his life over that stone, or so the story goes. He hadn't shared how, but I assumed that it had something to do with the person he had won it from. Anyway, Uncle Frank brought it home and hid it so that no one could steal it. The only problem was that he didn't tell anyone where he put it before he died, so if the legend is real and the diamond is hidden, no one knows where it is. They said it was called The Pink Diamond, so the legend is known as, The Legend..."

Heather joined in, "...of the Pink Diamond. So do you think that the legend is real?"

"I really don't know. I haven't heard anything about it since I was a child. All I know is, I used to have treasure hunts with my friends and we tried to find the diamond."

"Where did you look?"

Nikki shrugged. "Oh, I don't know…just everywhere. Everywhere but the attic. We weren't allowed up there."

"So did you look outside, too?"

"We tried, but my mother wouldn't let us dig. She was afraid that we would ruin her garden." Nikki smiled at the memory.

Heather broke out laughing. "I could just see you guys trying to dig on all of those acres."

Nikki giggled. "No, just underneath the gazebo. We just knew that it was there."

"It sounds like you guys must've had a great childhood living there."

Nikki smiled wistfully. "Yeah. I did, now that I think about it. There were things to do every season. I especially liked Christmas."

"So, what do you do at Christmas? Does the town do anything special?" Heather was really enjoying learning more about Harrot Reef. As many times as she had been here, she had never heard the whole story about the manor. She had never been there during this time of year so she was interested to hear how the town celebrated Christmas.

"Yeah, ever since I can remember, the township has had a huge tree brought in to the park every year. You saw it when we went to the sheriff's department. It's in the middle of the town square. Well, they decorate it with lights and special ornaments. On Christmas Eve the whole town comes to watch them light it up. They close Kelly Hill down to traffic for the night too and residents put on a Dickens' Christmas fair. The street has a contest to see which house has the best decorations. Visitors come from all around the county to watch Christmas skits in the street, while neighborhood kids and adults alike, dress in clothing of the era and walk up and down Kelly Hill while singing carols. The house at the end of the street always has a special display with Santa Claus and his elves greeting the children and handing out candy canes.

"That sounds like fun! Maybe we can take part in it. You know, sing carols or something."

Nikki looked up from her plate. She couldn't believe that Heather wanted to go. *She* certainly didn't.

Heather saw the look on Nikki's face. "I think that it might do us both good."

Nikki looked away thoughtfully. "Maybe."

Martha came over with their check. "Was it as good as it used to be Nikki?"

"Better." Nikki smiled.

"You know Miranda is working in here part-time now?"

"Miranda? Your daughter, Miranda?" Nikki was surprised. "Miranda was in high school the last time that I saw her."

"Just how old do you think she is?"

"She couldn't be more than 16."

Martha laughed. "Try 19."

"You're kidding! I remember when she was in braces"

"Well, her teeth are beautiful!"

"I would love to see her again," Nikki said.

"You just missed her. She works from at 8:00 a.m. to 12:00 p.m.. She sometimes works the evening shift, as well. She starts at 4:00 p.m. and she closes at 10:00 p.m.."

"Does she work on Saturdays?" Nikki asked. "We have to come down here anyway. Maybe we can come and see her."

"For the next two weeks, she will be working more since it's Christmas and she's out of school. She will be working all day tomorrow. I need her help, especially during the rushes. I only have one other waiter and, to tell you the truth, he is not worth what I pay him."

"Why don't you get someone else?"

"Because anybody else would want more money. Miranda works cheaper."

The three women laughed. Nikki and Heather bundled up in their coats, scarves, and gloves, and said their goodbyes before braving the freezing weather.

Heather pulled the car door shut, while Nikki flipped the heater on full blast.

"Where to now?"

"Let's go to Abel's to pick up groceries. Aunt Lynn's pantry is a little short on food."

Nikki was surprised that Aunt Lynn wasn't more prepared, but then again, she didn't know, until Wednesday, that Nikki and Heather would be coming before Christmas.

****

Nikki and Heather hurried into Abel's Groceries to pick up some milk, bread, eggs and cheese, and of course coffee, and walked to the checkout.

"Well, hi, Nikki! Long time no see."

Nikki looked up to see her old nemesis, Janet Davis. One thing about Janet, she was consistent. She was always jealous of Nikki when they were in high school. Nikki always got better grades and had nicer clothes than Janet. The fact that more people liked Nikki always enraged Janet. In fact, everything about Nikki got under Janet's skin.

The only good thing that Nikki could say about Janet is that she introduced Nikki to her brother, Tom, quite by chance. He was so different from his sister. Tom was kind, gentle and sincere. Nikki went out with him for a while, but she felt that he wanted too much from her relationship-wise. Instead, he ended up being her best friend during high school.

"Hi, Janet. How are you?"

Janet started to ring up the groceries. "I'm great. I married Jeff Koll...you remember Jeff. He was the quarterback for two years running." She barely took a breath before adding, "We have two kids, both in the most expensive preschool in the area."

Heather rolled her eyes towards the ceiling. She saw that Nikki's whole demeanor changed, and Heather knew from experience that if she didn't get her out of there, Nikki would uncharacteristically go off on this spoiled witch.

"How are your brothers?"

"You mean Tom and Brian? Oh," Janet flipped her hand as though she was chasing a bug away, "they're okay. You know, always complaining about something. Just like a man, am I right, ladies?" She flashed her insincere smile at them, as she bagged up the groceries. "Speak of the devil…"

Nikki looked up to see her old boyfriend and best friend from school standing in the doorway.

"Nikki? Nikki, is that you?" Tom rushed over to her, and threw his arms around her. "Oh my gosh! I didn't know that you were in town. Well, of course you would be." He lowered his voice, "I'm sorry about Lynn. You know that she was like a mother to me."

Nikki's eyes cast down to the floor. She was trying not to cry again. She just wanted to go home and sit in front of the fireplace and eat a huge banana split, her absolute favorite comfort food. She was tired of crying, tired of listening to Janet try to play one-upmanship, tired of everything.

"We were coming next week to spend Christmas with her, but she called and wanted us to come early. When I got here…" she hesitated, "…I found her in the library."

Tom held on to Nikki's arms and bent to look her in the eye.

"Anything I can do? You know I'll do anything for you, Nikki."

Nikki just shook her head. She dare not say anything for fear of breaking down right there in Abel's Grocery.

"Thanks, Tom, but I'm fine. I've got Heather helping me." She indicated Heather, who was a step behind her.

Tom raised his brown eyes to face Heather's beautiful aqua eyes. "Oh hi, Heather. How are you?" He reached to clasp Heather's outstretched hand.

"I'm fine," Heather said automatically.

Nikki cleared her throat. "Well, we should go. Heather and I want to get to the bakery before it closes."

Tom followed the two friends out to their car.

As he held the door for Nikki to get in he said in a low voice, "If you need anything, please call." He handed her a slip of paper. "Here is my new phone number. Feel free to call…anytime."

The snowflakes started to fall and settled on his chestnut brown hair. He reached down and kissed her on the cheek. "It really is good to see you, Nikki."

With that, he closed the door and picked his way through the icy parking lot, back to the store.

"He is so nice, Nikki. I really do like him."

"We dated in high school until he wanted more than I did. Come to think of it," Nikki said dreamily, "I almost didn't meet him at all. If it wasn't for the car accident that killed mom and Dad, I probably would've gone to high school back in California. But then it happened and Aunt Lynn sent for me to live with her here; I met his sister, who in turn introduced me to Tom."

"Yeah, I know. It's strange how one event can change your whole path instantly."

****

The last stop of the day, was the bakery. As they walked to the door, Heather noticed the cute sign that was dangling from heavy chains. It was made out of an old plank of driftwood, painted sky blue. Two fat cats were etched on it and the words 'The Fat Cat Bakery' were scrawled below. The building was light blue clapboard, with a dark blue and white striped awning. In the window, was a neon sign that blinked O P E N in red letters.

When they opened the door, a gust of warm air that smelled of fresh baked bread hit their senses and drew them to the counter like a magnet.

The girl who came out from the back room was slight in build. She was in her early twenties and she had a foul disposition that exuded from her. The girl could be quite beautiful if she would lose the attitude and about half of her makeup. Her bright blue eyes were big and appeared full of innocence, which was as fake as the fake eyelashes she was wearing, of that, Heather was certain. Her short black hair was spiked and was peppered with a bright blue streak on the left side of her head. The clothes that she wore were as dark as her attitude. Her black leather pants were adorned with silver studs. She wore a men's black sleeveless T-shirt and topped all of this off with a dirty white apron. She looked as though she wanted to be anywhere but there.

"Yeah, what can I get you?" Her attitude was as rough as she looked.

"Hi. We need a loaf of bread and can we get some of those cinnamon rolls," Heather said, indicating the iced rolls in the display case.

"How many do ya want?"

"Two, please."

The girl grunted, grabbed the cinnamon rolls and a loaf of bread and stuffed them into a bag.

As she rang up the order on an old-fashioned cash register, her father Gene, who is also the owner of the bakery, came out whistling a nameless tune.

"Hey, Nikki!" He rounded the counter in three giant steps and embraced Nikki in a bear hug.

"Hi Gene. You remember my friend Heather."

"Sure I do. I could never forget someone so beautiful." Gene winked as he shook Heather's hand. "It's been a long time. I believe the last time I saw you was in the Summer, wasn't it?"

Heather smiled warmly. *I had forgotten how charming this guy is.* "Yes, I was here in August enjoying your delicious cinnamon rolls. I got home and found that I had gained five pounds. I'm sure it was from all of those rolls. You make the best I've ever tasted. In fact, we bought some for tomorrow morning."

"Well, I'm glad you like them." Gene noticed the bag that she was holding. "It looks like you've already paid for those, but the next rolls are on the house."

Turning to Nikki, he said, "And how are you holding up, sweetie?"

Nikki blinked the tears away. "I'm okay," she lied. "I still can't believe that she's gone."

Gene quickly said, "I'm so sorry. Lynn was a big part of this town, and she will be missed."

The girl behind the counter mumbled just loud enough to hear, "You mean her money will be missed."

Nikki gasped audibly.

Gene turned on his daughter and Heather thought that he would lose control. "Nikki, I'm sorry for Roxey's rudeness. I'm sure what she meant to say is she was sorry for your loss. Right, Roxey?"

It didn't sound very sincere when Roxey grumbled, "Yeah, I guess so." She sighed, rolled her eyes and disappeared into the back.

The tension that filled the air seemed to vanish with her.

Gene turned to Heather to explain. "Roxey's mother died when she was five. I couldn't take care of a five year old by myself, so I sent her to live with her aunt. Then when she became eighteen, she accessed all of the money that her mother had willed to her and struck out on her own to live in New York. She met a guy and to make a long story short, he took her for all that she had. She came back here penniless. Roxey still *loves* him," Gene rolled his eyes, "even though he tricked her out of every cent her mother left to her. That was what we were discussing before you came in. She is blaming me for the breakup because I never approved of him. Everything is my fault. I guess that's what it means to be a parent."

Nikki's mind flashed back to the similarities between her background and Roxey's. Sure, she was devastated when Mom and Dad died when she was ten years old, but she felt grateful that she had Aunt Lynn and Harrot Reef.

"Well, you'll get it straightened out, Gene." Trying to lighten the mood, Nikki turned to Heather. "Did I ever tell you that Gene used to date my aunt a long time ago...and he still has that old charm, don't you?" Nikki elbowed him and grinned.

Gene laughed so hard that his whole body seemed to shake.

"That was a long, long time ago. Back when I was about 50 pounds lighter and had more hair."

Heather and Nikki both smiled.

Nikki picked the baked goods up from the counter turned to Gene, gave him a quick peck on the cheek and turned to leave.

"We'll see you later."

Walking to the car, Heather asked, "What's for dinner?"

"A surprise."

****

That afternoon, Nikki was lost in a book, while Heather was in the office writing.

Nikki looked at the clock. *5:00 p.m.—I'm actually hungry again. I'd better start dinner.* Harry followed Nikki into the kitchen and sat in front of the Magic Cupboard.

"Trill."

"Oh, alright. I'll feed you first."

Nikki added a little smoked salmon flavored wet food to his dry and put it in front of him. She took out a pan, splashed in a little olive oil and about a half of a tablespoon of butter to keep the oil from burning. She added diced onions, browned them. Then she drained off all of the excess oil and butter and was about to add some hamburger into the pan when Heather came in.

Inhaling the sweet aroma of red onions, Heather remarked, "Gosh, that smells good."

"It's only hamburger and onions. You were gone for a long time. Where did you go? Did you get your article finished?"

"No. I went in to check out the library and picked up a book. You know me, once I've picked up a good book, I have a hard time putting it down. Do you know how many Agatha Christie books are in Aunt Lynn's library?"

Nikki smiled and nodded. "A copy of every Christie book ever written...yeah well, Aunt Lynn always did love a good mystery, and she used to say that nobody writes one as good as Agatha. Aunt Lynn used to call her "the queen of mysteries". Suddenly, Nikki felt the emptiness in her heart that simply talking about Aunt Lynn gave her. A tear slid down her cheek. She silently thanked God that Heather was behind her and couldn't see the emotional moment that she had just suffered through.

"Hey, is it me, or has the town changed since last Summer? Heather asked.

Nikki snapped out of her reverie. "You mean physically...like the town itself?"

"No, well it is different that way, too, but I figure a lot of that has to do with the Christmas decorations. What I'm talking about is more the mood of the people. They seem...I don't know...just different somehow."

"I know what you mean; it *does* seem different. It really feels strange, oppressive."

Nikki cracked open an egg, a reminder of her breaking heart and she blinked back the tears again. She shook her head to free her mind of the grief-stricken thoughts and went back to her almost mindless task of preparing dinner.

Heather came up behind Nikki. Scrunching her nose up, she asked, "What *are* you cooking?"

"Joe's special." In went the last two ingredients, mushrooms and spinach. "You want to grab the salad out of the refrigerator?"

Nikki dished out two healthy-sized servings of the hamburger mixture and brought the plates to the table.

"Drink?" Heather had her hand on an open bottle of Cabernet. Nikki nodded her head.

Heather looked at her dinner plate. She still wasn't sure about the strange concoction.

"What's in this?"

While eating her first bite of dinner, Nikki said, "Oh, just eat it. It won't kill you. Tomorrow is your turn to cook."

There was silence as the two friends ate; Nikki was gulping down her Joe's Special while Heather picked at her salad.

"So, what have you got planned?" Nikki asked.

"What?"

"Dinner...tomorrow. Hello? Are you in there?" Nikki smiled.

Heather shook her head to clear the cobwebs.

"Sorry. Yeah, dinner. I don't know. Maybe my famous chili or spaghetti."

"I vote for chili!"

Heather tentatively took a bite of her hamburger based meal. Her expression immediately changed. "Mm, this is delicious."

"That will teach you to eat with your eyes. What were you lost in thought about?"

Heather chased down the food with a sip of wine. "When?"

"Just a few minutes ago," said Nikki.

"Oh. I was just thinking about Janet, your-old-boyfriend-Tom's sister."

"What about her?"

Heather looked at Nikki quizzically. "What is with you two? Is she jealous of you or what?"

"I think that she is jealous of my relationship with her brother, although I have no idea why. I had nothing against her, she just ran in another circle of people, all of them as stuck-up as she. We tolerated each other, she even acknowledged my existence, until after she introduced me to Tom. Then her treatment of me became worse than it was before. Ever since high school, she has been trying to prove that she is better than me at everything and she hasn't changed a bit, as you saw today."

"Boy, I'll say. How can she be so different from her brother?" Heather stuffed her mouth with some of the hamburger mixture.

"I don't know. That's a good question. Tom always said she was a "Daddy's girl". I don't know, maybe her dad spoiled her. She was the only girl in the family."

"Janet mentioned Brian. How come I've never met him?"

"He was in the service until two months ago. We kept in touch by mail while he was in the Middle East for a while until he was stationed in Germany. Before the service, he was in California to go to U.C. Berkeley. He's a sweet guy, a little on the shy side compared to his brother and sister."

Nikki wiped her mouth. As she stood up she said, "I'll have to introduce him to you. I think you'll like him."

"I'd like that," Heather said as she helped Nikki clear the table.

After finishing dinner, Nikki wandered into the parlor, and sat down on the silk covered couch.

Heather came in ten minutes later in her pajamas, robe and fur lined slippers.

"Nikki, why are you sitting here in the dark?"

Nikki was jolted from her thoughts. "Hmm? Oh, I'm just enjoying the fire."

The women silently gazed at the flames as they finished the pudding they had for dessert.

Harry sauntered in to the room and announced himself with a loud meow. He strutted over to Nikki, and head butted her hand.

"Look at that!" Heather smiled.

Nikki looked down and smiled. "He must miss Aunt Lynn too." She stooped to pick him up. "Aunt Lynn always said that he is a special cat. He can make you feel better just by petting him." Nikki nuzzled the big cat.

"Don't they say that about all cats though?"

Nikki smiled. "I suppose so, but I like to think that Harry has extra special powers. When I visited when I was little, he would follow me around, almost like he was watching over me. Aunt Lynn would call him her 'elite baby-sitter'. She used to say that when I was under Harry's watchful eye, she knew that I wouldn't get into trouble...that Harry wouldn't let anything or anyone harm me."

"He's just a cat, Nikki. How could he protect you from anything?"

Nikki's eyes went from the glazed-over effect that comes from remembering things of long ago, to a clear vision of the present.

"I don't know, but when Harry was around, it seemed that nothing went wrong."

"Until now." Heather immediately wished that she could take the words back.

Heather felt Nikki's eyes boring holes into her soul. She saw the pain that her statement had caused Nikki.

"I'm sorry. I shouldn't have said that."

"No. It's true. It makes you wonder, if Harry had this 'charm or power', why didn't he use it that night?"

"What do you suppose happened?" Heather was curious. If nobody around town had it out for her, then why did she die, she thought to herself?

"Oh, I don't know." Nikki seemed to be in her own world for a few minutes, then she broke the silence. "Maybe it was her heart. Although, I doubt it. Like I said earlier, my family doesn't have a history of heart problems."

"Is there anything else that you can think of that might have caused her death?"

Nikki thought a minute. "No, nothing. So, you can see why I'm thinking that it had to be foul play."

They fell silent, staring into the fire, each with their own thoughts. Nikki was finding a little peace as she petted Harry.

Heather heaved herself up. "I'm going to make hot cocoa. Do you want anything from the kitchen?"

Nikki shook her head and then changed her mind. "I'll have some cocoa too, please."

Before she knew it, Heather was standing in front of her, holding a mug of steamy cocoa for her. Nikki accepted it with a quiet "Thank you", and continued with her thoughts. Suddenly, she jumped up and left the room.

"Nikki, where are you going?"

"I'm just getting my laptop."

Nikki came back to the parlor with newfound energy.

"What are you doing?"

"Just a second."

Nikki impatiently waited while the computer booted up, then she opened a browser. She searched for Pu-erh tea.

"I don't know why I didn't think of this before."

"Think of what before? What are you looking up?"

"I think that Aunt Lynn told me that the Pu-erh tea had a very small bit of arsenic in it. I looked it up once on the Internet and found several articles about the tea, a few even told about people dying from it."

Nikki found what she was looking for. In the cases that she read about, the tea was bought in California; San Francisco, to be exact.

"That's it!"

"What is it? Come on, Nikki. Let me in on the brilliant idea you have got."

"The articles that made it on the Internet were about people who got sick and/or died from drinking the tea. Although, the tea that was tampered with came from California, who's to say it hasn't made its way here. It says in here that they think that it was tainted with arsenic, but they couldn't be certain because the tea contains a small amount of arsenic already. But, let's suppose that someone gave the untainted tea to Aunt Lynn, and tried to pass it off as accidently tainted by the company that put it out."

"That's a big supposition, Nikki."

"Not really. Everyone knew that Aunt Lynn always drank exotic teas. Her friends gave her different types of teas all of the time. So, let's say someone bought it in one of the health food stores in the area... say that person was the killer. All that person would have to do is pay in cash so there wouldn't be any record, and add extra arsenic to it."

"Nikki, I think that you are clutching at straws," Heather said.

"I think that we'd better wait for the autopsy before jumping to conclusions." Heather suggested.

"Hmm. Okay", Nikki was continuing to quickly type on the keyboard.

"What are you doing now?"

"Just checking my email."

"I'm going to bed. You coming, or are you going to stay up awhile?" Heather was tired, which made sense considering all that she and Nikki had been through today. Nikki should be tired, too.

"In a minute." Nikki's head was bent over her computer as she concentrated on an email from her publisher reminding her that the deadline for her book was looming ahead. She shook her head, powered off the computer and went up to bed.

Even though Nikki's room was large, it was inviting. One might say that it was even cozy. Victorian in style, the walls were covered with maroon and gold silk. Pictures of Harrot Reef from years ago covered the wall. Her bed was covered with sheets that were white as snow and a maroon comforter with lace around the edges. The drapes were made from the finest white silk that Nikki had seen. In between the two windows was an antique carved dressing table with a beautifully detailed mirror. The sitting area was located on the other side of the room and logs were already placed on the grate, ready for a blazing fire to be started. The regal antique fainting couch matched the maroon headboard on the bed.

Nikki soaked in the elegance of the room. The silk on the walls reminded her of how the very rich lived in the early 1900's. The only thing that Aunt Lynn had changed in this room was to enlarge it by knocking down a wall between two rooms, and adding the white touches. Everything was just as it had been when she was a little girl and she called it her own.

Nikki peeled off her jeans and sweater and slipped into her nightgown. Pulling the comforter off the bed, book in hand, she tiptoed to the couch in front of the fire.

Opening up her book, she found where she had left off when reading this afternoon. She read the first paragraph and realized that she didn't know what she had just read, so she read it again. Still unable to retain comprehension, she became frustrated and threw the book across the room.

"Oh Aunt Lynn...who did this to you?!" She hung her head and cried herself to sleep.

Chapter 4

Saturday, December 8th

Nikki awakened when she heard a man's voice, deep, but almost at a whisper. "Don't worry. I'll take care of her." Nikki opened her eyes. It must've been a dream.

The fire was out and her nightgown, although flannel, was still too thin to keep her warm, even with the thick comforter. Teeth chattering, she quickly donned her jeans and the sweater from the night before, and dragged a brush through her long blond hair. She opened the door to find Harry sitting there with an expectant look on his face.

Nikki picked him up and he looked at her with love, and softly caressed her cheek with a giant paw. "Good morning, Harry. Are you hungry?"

With that, he sprang from her arms and raced downstairs. Laughing, Nikki exclaimed, "Oh, now I see. You just wanted food, not love!"

Nikki followed the aroma of freshly brewed coffee downstairs to the kitchen. This room was one of the rooms that Aunt Lynn had renovated. Its high vaulted ceiling made the room look even bigger than it really was. From the sink, the view included the beautiful gazebo and the ocean beyond. The wood on the cabinets was blond. An elegant, modern light fixture hung over an island in the middle of the room. The island had a vegetable sink on one side and a inlaid electric stove on the other. On one end of the island was a glass table top that served as a breakfast table. The counters that ran along the cupboards were of yellow and black granite, polished to a sheen.

"Do you want some coffee?" Heather was pouring a cup without waiting for an answer.

"Mmm." Nikki savored the first sip of the rich chocolate flavored coffee. "I think this is my favorite kind of coffee."

"Of course, it is. You and your chocolate. Honestly Nikki, I have never seen anyone love chocolate more than you."

Harry meowed to let them know that he was waiting for his breakfast.

"Oh, alright! Anybody would think we never feed you." Heather opened the Magic Cupboard that he was sitting in front of, begging for breakfast.

Nikki sat at the breakfast table, while Heather unwrapped the two huge homemade cinnamon rolls they had picked up from the bakery yesterday. She joined Nikki at the table, licking her fingers after she put her friend's plate in front of her.

"Was there a man in here?" Nikki asked, pulling a bite-sized piece of off her roll.

"When?"

"This morning. When I woke up. I heard a man's voice. A sort of husky whispering outside my bedroom door."

"You must have been dreaming. There was nobody here but you, me and Harry."

Nikki shook her head and muttered, "Weird." After taking a sip of coffee, Nikki asked, "You know that girl who helped us at the bakery?"

"Oh, you mean Roxey?"

"Yep. She dropped out of school in her junior year of high school to be with her boyfriend. He swooped into town and carried her off to New York city. They set up house for a while, then one night, he left in the middle of the night without saying a word. Like her dad Gene said, he sadly took all of her inheritance that she received from her mother."

"Since she had no money, she came back to Harrot Reef to live with her father and started working at his bakery to pay the rent. She had a reputation of being a 'bad girl' before she left town, but now she's a pariah around here."

"Well, I can see why. The white makeup and black lipstick and nail polish. I'm usually not so judgmental, but all those piercings grossed even me out. And the eye make-up!" Heather shivered in repulsion.

"That's the fashion now." Nikki shook her head. "Go figure."

After a long pause, Heather changed the subject. "I hate to bring this up, but do you know what Lynn wanted to do as far as a funeral?"

"Aunt Lynn and I talked about it a while back. She didn't want a funeral. She thought that it would be too hard on me. That's Aunt Lynn, always thinking of others. Anyway, I talked her into a small memorial for those who need closure. I guess I should start arranging that, huh?"

"Yeah, it might be a good thing. Where will you have it?" Heather asked.

"I don't know what she wanted. What do you think about having it here? The house is big enough."

"That's really up to you." Heather said, then she popped a piece of cinnamon bun in her mouth. "Would it be too much work for you, though?" When Nikki gave her a confused look, Heather continued, "I mean, you'd be adding a few more "To Dos" to the long list of things that you already have to do."

"Not really. I can hire someone to come in and help with setting things up and even have the food catered by the deli here in town."

"Do you want to wait until after Christmas?" Heather asked.

"No. Aunt Lynn loved Christmas. She would want us to go ahead with it so there's no cloud over this meaningful holiday."

"What about an obituary? Lynn was so popular that I'm sure the whole town would like to come to the memorial. You need to tell them where and when it is," Heather reminded Nikki.

"I didn't even think of that. Do I have to wait until they release the body?"

"Why? I think that, as long as we're memorializing her and not having a funeral, we can do it anytime. Let's see. It's Saturday. Do you think that we can have everything ready in two weeks?" Heather suggested.

"If we start today. I just don't know where to begin."

Heather pulled out her cell from her pocket. "Let's Google it."

Heather spent the next half hour telling Nikki what they have to do and in what order, while Nikki wrote the tasks down. At last, when they were through, they had a list of more than a dozen things.

Nikki read through the list again and began to cross off unnecessary tasks. "We don't need to worry about some of these, like the location. We have already figured that one out. And we said that the deli can cater it."

"Sure, but we have to plan the menu."

"Oh yeah. I don't suppose that I could get together with David, the owner, and tell him to do whatever?" Nikki asked, hopefully.

Heather smiled slightly as she shook her head. "No. I'm afraid not. He'll need some sort of direction."

"I suppose you're right. So, where do we begin?"

Heather looked down at the list on the computer. "Number one says, 'Decide on a theme'. Well, I don't know about that, so let's go on to number two."

Nikki read from her list, "'Choose a location'. Well, that's done. Number three is to select the date. Do you honestly think a week is enough time? I think we should give it two weeks, at least."

Heather said, "Okay, one week from tomorrow?"

"Hmm. That sounds better. I guess I should write the obituary so that we can get it in the paper today."

Nikki's pen hovered over the notebook in front of her. After a few moments, she threw it down so hard that the pen bounced off the pad and landed on the floor. She crossed her arms on top of the notepad and lay her head atop her arms. She cried softly into her sweater.

"You can do this, Nikki," Heather reassured her. Heather picked up the pen and handed it to Nikki. "Just keep it short."

After half an hour of stops and starts, Nikki had written a simple obituary for Lynn.

Heather tore it off the pad, handed Nikki her purse and rushed her out of the door.

****

It was snowing so hard that, even though the roads had been cleared and salted, Nikki had difficulty controlling the car. She dropped her speed way down and flipped the windshield wipers on high. The two women didn't speak.

When they finally got to the newspaper office, a young girl that Nikki didn't recognize was standing behind the counter. She took the piece of paper that Heather offered and read it.

Turning to Heather, "Nikki?"

Heather corrected her. "No, this is Nikki. I'm just a friend."

The girl looked at Nikki with sincere sympathy. "I'm so sorry, Nikki."

"Do I know you?" Nikki asked.

"No, but your aunt has told me so much about you that I feel I've known you forever. I'm Ruby." She reached across the counter to shake Nikki's hand.

"Well, thank you, Ruby."

Heather pulled on Nikki's jacket. She was looking through the window.

"O'Neil." Heather whispered.

Nikki turned around. Sure enough, O'Neil and Deputy Holloway were standing on the front steps, right beside the door. Nikki and Heather couldn't avoid him if they wanted to get out of the building. *I didn't do anything. I don't have to avoid him.*

Taking her time, Nikki turned back toward the counter and retrieved her checkbook from her purse. "How much do I owe you?" Nikki wrote the check, tore it off, and then showed Ruby her I. D.

Without turning around , Nikki asked Heather, "Is he still there?"

"Yep."

"What do you suppose he wants now?"

"I don't know, but he's giving me the creeps. It's like he's always lurking in the background."

"Well, here goes nothing."

Aunt Lynn always told her that you catch more flies with honey than you do vinegar. Although, Nikki always wondered what you would want with flies. She plastered a smile on her face and walked through the door.

"Have you found something?"

The sheriff grinned and spit out his toothpick. *What a disgusting habit!*

"You could say that. You need to come downtown with us." He was demanding and yet he was getting some pleasure out of whatever it was that he found.

Nikki looked questionably at the deputy, and he averted his eyes. Something was up, and it wasn't good. The snow had stopped falling, yet she felt the chill in the air.

"Why do you want me to go with you?"

"You are a suspect in the murder of Lynn Johnson." O'Neil spat.

"What?!"

The two women were astonished at the notion that anyone would think that Nikki could kill anybody, let alone her own aunt.

Nikki looked at the deputy with pleading eyes. Again, he avoided looking at her.

Nikki gave Heather the car keys. "Call Mr. Wilson, my aunt's attorney. His number is in her date book by the phone. He'll know what to do."

"I'll get you out as soon as possible." Heather said reassuringly, then she threw a sour look at the sheriff, who just sneered and walked away, dragging Nikki after him.

O'Neil shoved her into the car, without taking care to guard her head against bumping it. As a result, she hit the roof of the car so hard that she was sure that she would have a lump and a possible black eye later. Holloway saw this and flinched at the pain that Nikki must have felt.

Sheriff O'Neil purposely drove below the speed limit, taking joy in the looks they received from the townspeople and the shop owners on the way to the City Hall. While he had a look of triumph, Deputy Holloway had one of chagrin. Nikki was not embarrassed as the sheriff had hoped, but in shock.

Once in the parking space designated especially for the department's vehicle, O'Neil opened the rear door and yanked Nikki out. He led her slowly into the building, making sure that everyone on the street could see that the only Johnson left in town was being hauled into jail. Within a hour, almost all of the townspeople knew that Nikki Johnson, the last living relative of the family who founded the town of Harrot Reef, was accused of murdering her own aunt.

****

Deputy Holloway's eyes followed the sheriff and Nikki as they went into the room that Heather had been interrogated in. After the door closed, O'Neil turned to Nikki. He looked pleased with himself when he saw that her eyes were filled with fear.

The sheriff gestured for her to sit on one of the cold, hard metal chairs. She glanced around and saw a room that was painted with the ugliest green color that she'd ever seen. It was peeling off the walls to expose an even nastier grey.

Nikki sat, perched on the chair, trying not to sit back on a wad of dried gum. O'Neil sauntered up to the dented, gray table with a satisfied grin on his face. He looked down at her, removed the toothpick from his mouth.

"The autopsy was done this morning. Guess what we found?"

Nikki looked at him anxiously. "What?"

"Arsenic."

"Aunt Lynn used to drink this disgusting tea everyday for her blood pressure. I know that it has a trace of arsenic in it. Could that be the source?"

"Now isn't that interesting?" O'Neil was gloating now.

"What?"

"That you should know a thing like that. That could answer a lot of questions."

"Like what, sheriff?"

"Like the fact that you knew that this tea had arsenic in it. You also knew that your aunt took it daily."

"Yeah. So?"

"So, what was to keep you from adding an extra little bit to keep her sick and then swoop into town and feed her the final dose?" O'Neil paused a moment to let it sink in. "Like I told you last night, we'll know more when the toxicology report comes in. That will be the last nail in your coffin."

O'Neil turned his chair around, and straddled it. He glared at Nikki.

Nikki was shaking, not with fear, but with anger. She wanted to slap that grin off of his flabby, sweaty face. She knew this had nothing to do with her and everything to do with her mom choosing her dad over him all those years ago.

"I just want to warn you that you are my chief suspect, heck, my only suspect as of now. So, for the safety of the town, I'm locking you up."

Nikki knew that O'Neil didn't really think that she killed her Aunt Lynn, but he was enjoying keeping her locked up in his jail, and he would probably keep her here up until the very second that the law said he had to let her go.

****

"Jonathan Wilson."

"Yes, Mr. Wilson. My name is Heather Murphy, I'm a friend of Nikki Johnson." Heather breathed into the phone.

"Yes, I heard that there was trouble at Harrot Reef Manor. I'm so sorry about Lynn. What can I do for you?"

"They've taken Nikki in on a murder charge! Mr. Wilson, I know that Nikki didn't do it! I was with her...I mean, we found Lynn together! Can you help?!"

"Pretty dirty move arresting on a Saturday. They know she can't get out until Monday." He paused for a moment. "Okay, Miss Murphy. The first thing you need to do is stay calm. You won't do Nikki any good if you are upset. Next, I'll call down and talk to the judge and see if we can get the bail hearing set for Monday. We are poker buddies, although I wouldn't trust him with a plug nickel. On top of that, he is a tough nut to crack. Still, he's a darn good judge and he might listen to me. What number can I reach you at?"

"My cell is 212-555-1373."

"Okay. Stay by the phone. I'll call the judge and find out when the hearing is going to be and then call you back."

After she clicked off her cell, Heather heated up some coffee from this morning. She sat at the kitchen island and thought about the mess that they were in. Harry jumped up on her lap, head butted her hand and started to purr. Heather petted the cat, thinking of how she was going to get the money for bail. She could put up her condo and she can try to have Nikki out by Monday afternoon. A peace came over her. Yes, that's what they would do.

Suddenly, the silence was broken by the loud ring of the telephone. "Mr. Wilson?"

"Yes. The judge agreed to Monday morning. Do you have the money to bail her out now? If you have to wait for someone to wire the money, the soonest we can get her out is Monday afternoon."

Heather didn't have to think twice about it. "Yes, I can do it, but since it is Saturday, it will have to wait until Monday morning."

"That will be fine. Nikki should be okay over the weekend. She might need some personal items."

"That was my next move. Thank you Mr. Wilson."

They said their goodbyes and rang off.

****

"Spread the word. The gang needs to get together for a very important meeting at The Fence at sundown," Harry called to Dewey.

Harry watched as Dewey sprinted across the street. He was the fastest in Harry's gang. When he let loose, all that you could see was a black streak flying. If you were in his path, you'd better step aside. And he was smart. For a young cat, not even a year old, he caught on fast, better than most. Of course, most cats are exceptionally smart, especially when compared to their counterparts. Oh, Harry had a few friends that were dogs; darned handy creatures, but extremely intelligent they are not. Well, at least in his opinion.

Harry vanished from the front yard, and in a flash was beside Heather doing his best to calm her down. He knew that his gang would not let him down. Nikki would come home; Heather would make sure of that, and then he and the others would take over. Harry had a few tricks that he saved just for occasions like this. Well, not exactly like this. He had never had one of his charges thrown in jail for killing another. That's just nuts! Harry watched Nikki grow up.

He knew that she could never hurt anybody. Besides, Johnsons don't hurt Johnsons. It's just not done.

He rubbed on Heather's leg and, when she smiled at him, he leaped onto her lap and started to purr, telling her, in his own special way, that everything was going to be alright. After all, Harry was there and he would take care of it.

****

A half hour went by...still no word from Heather. Nikki knew that she would get out of jail, but what next?

What's to keep O'Neil from building a bogus case against her? He hated her father, and by extension, the whole Johnson family because Stephen Johnson had asked her mother to marry him. When Mom had said yes, that was the end of Grady O'Neil's chances to win her heart. He had fought to beat her dad and lost. To his way of thinking, the Johnsons always came out on top.

But no more. The fat, sweaty man came sauntering in, proud as a peacock. "So, how did you do it?"

"I...did...not...do...*anything!* Why would I kill my own aunt? She was *my flesh and blood!* I loved her, but then you wouldn't know anything about love, would you, sheriff?"

O'Neil's fat neck and face turned beet-red. He spit out the toothpick that he was chewing on.

"Now listen here, little lady..."

"Don't you, 'little lady' me! You have nothing on me. No evidence that I did this. Why are you taking the chance of a lawsuit? Do you really hate my family that much?"

"I have enough to hold you on suspicion of murder. The coroner's initial exam showed several signs of arsenic poisoning, such as Mees' lines, the little white lines under the fingernails, and skin bumps. Oh, yeah. He also said something about her skin being discolored. Right now, I'm holding you because I think that maybe you might just have come up here to ask for some money. And maybe your aunt said no. Maybe you had a huge fight, and..."

"And what? I left in the middle of it to fix her some arsenic on the rocks?"

"We'll be certain when we get the toxicology report back. The law states that I can hold you 48 hours. 'Til then, you sit tight, little missy. Oh, and sleep well." He grinned his malicious grin as he deliberately slammed and locked the cell door.

****

It seemed like days instead of just an hour or so before Nikki saw Heather again. The guard unlocked the cell door for Heather to enter into Nikki's cell.

"The deputy came by and told me that O'Neil intended on keeping you here the full 48 hours allowed by law." Heather smiled at the guard as he unlocked the cell door for her.

"I know! How can they? They don't have any evidence. It could have been anyone."

Heather put her hand up. She needed to keep Nikki calm....to let her know that things will be okay. "Greg also said that he can't hold you unless he finds some solid proof. He's sure that all of the tests will prove you to be innocent. The toxicology report won't be in for weeks, especially with Christmas. They have to send it to Greendale because they don't have the equipment here. Greendale is backed up with requests."

Heather swung the big, black, canvas bag on the bench.

"I brought your book, which I found down on your bedroom floor. What happened there?"

Nikki looked up at her meekly. "I got a little upset last night."

"Okay...well, I also brought some personal items, toothbrush, toothpaste, hair brush and makeup."

Nikki looked at Heather incredulously. "Makeup? In here?"

"You never know. Oh, and just in case they let you change, I brought you some clothes. I also have your notes for your manuscript, just to keep you out of trouble." She winked impishly.

"Thanks, Heather."

"Don't worry. We'll get you out of here soon."

"We'll?"

"The deputy and I."

Heather winked again and the officer that was standing at the door smirked as he unlocked the cell to let her out.

"Take it easy. We'll take care of it as soon as possible."

Then she was gone.

****

Heather was unlocking the door when she heard Nikki's phone ring. She knew that Nikki hadn't had time to get it before O'Neil hauled her off to jail. Heather shook her head. Just thinking about the situation made her see red again. Running into the kitchen, she tripped over Harry, who was basking in the only tiny pool of sunlight in the whole house on this cold winter's day.

"Harry!"

He looked up at her and, with a nonchalance that only a cat has, he blinked twice and opened his mouth to give way to a big yawn, stretched and went back to sleep.

Heather grabbed the phone on the fifth rang. "Hello?" she said, while trying to catch her breath.

"Hi, Nikki??"

"No. This is her friend. Nikki isn't here right now. Can I help you?" Heather could hear the tension in her voice, and self-consciously cleared her throat.

"Hi, Heather," Tom said cheerfully. "This is Tom. I'm calling to ask you and Nikki to dinner. My brother, Brian would be joining us."

"Well, like I said, Nikki isn't here."

Tom's voice abruptly changed. "Heather? What's the matter? Did something happen to Nikki?" His words ran together. It was clear that anxiety overcame Tom's cheerfulness.

Heather hesitated, trying to swallow the lump in her throat. In a small voice, which was uncharacteristic for her, "Nikki...Nikki is in jail, Tom."

"Jail? What in the blazes is she doing in jail?!"

"Sheriff O'Neil and his deputy took her away. She's wanted in connection with Lynn's death."

"Well, that's just plain stupid."

"I know, right? I called Lynn's lawyer and the bail hearing won't be until Monday morning. I can't do anything until Monday afternoon when I know just how much money I need to transfer from New York. Anyway, to answer your question about dinner, things are up in the air, as you can imagine. I'll have Nikki get back to you."

Before she lost control of all of her emotions, she rang off.

****

"Okay. Is everybody here?"

Harry was standing in the midst of all of the neighborhood cats. Dewey looked around the circle, counting them all...all except one. Ollie.

"Hey, Harry. Ollie's late again."

"His charge must have found the hole in the screen and fixed it again. He'll be here. I talked to him myself and he knows how important this one is," Harry said.

Out of all of their capers through the years, this might just be the toughest. After all, it's not everyday that a charge gets thrown into jail.

"What are we waiting for then?"

This came from the ever-impatient Jasper. He was a no-nonsense cat with a tough guy air about him. It probably came from spending his first year of his life on the streets. He was the gang's streetwise cat, able to see through all of the tricks. He learned at a very early age that, if you want to make it in this world, you have to be willing to play dirty. For all of his tenacity, there was one human who could wrap him around her little finger, his little guardian, Suzy.

Suzy was a ten year old girl who found him one blustery day, cold, hungry and worn out from a fight that he had been in with the neighborhood dog, Mike. The child had gently picked him up, cradled him in her arms, and took him home. Her mom cleaned up Jasper, fed him a dish of fresh salmon and fixed him a bed in front of the fireplace. Since then, he knew that he had a home to go to when he got hungry, cold or just needed to be held.

Harry cleared his throat and waited for all of the others to quiet down. "As all of you know, my charge died."

There were general sounds of sorrow all around. Harry held up his paw, quieting everyone down. "Thank you all. Anyway, my new charge is in jail for Lynn's murder and that's absolute nonsense. Some of you know Nikki. She wouldn't hurt a soul, right?"

The others were riled and each said their piece.

"It's that sheriff," Big Ron, a huge marmalade color tom yelled over all of the others. "He's had it out for your family, Harry, since I can remember."

O'Malley, Big Ron's twin said, "It's time somebody got rid of that nut bag."

"Yeah, he's caused enough trouble in our town."

With that, the voices were raised loud enough to alert the humans in the street.

Harry raised his paws again and called for quiet. Immediately, everyone obeyed. They all knew that Harry was in charge.

"Okay. Here's the situation. Nikki's in jail. I was hiding in the library the night they found her and I heard the sheriff telling the coroner at the crime scene that he was going to find some way to pin the whole thing on Nikki. So, even when she is released, O'Neil will be hounding her, trying to find evidence that will prove that she killed Lynn."

Little Bea, the smallest of them all, piped up in her small voice, "But she didn't kill her, did she?"

"No, of course not! Knowing O'Neil, he will plant the evidence himself," Harry answered.

"What do they have on her?" Alfie wanted to know.

"I don't know…yet. Dewey, Little Bea and Ollie will help me to find out."

Big Ron piped up. "Why only them? Why not use all of us."

The gang raised their voices again.

"Yeah! We want to help!"

"You will, by being our eyes and ears, but I need someone who's fast, someone who can cause a distraction, and someone who is small and can easily hide. That's Dewey, Ollie and Little Bea."

Upon hearing her name, Little Bea puffed up her chest and beamed all over.

Just then, Ollie rounded the corner, as fast as his legs could carry him. Ollie was the biggest member of the gang, even bigger than Harry. He was fluffy, which deceived all of the humans into thinking that he was a pushover. Ollie only had two faults, and both annoyed Harry to no end: he was a little overweight, which meant that he had trouble keeping up with the rest of them; and he was lazy. He would rather lie on his back and accept treats from his guardians than to explore like the other cats. One thing that Ollie was good at was creating diversions. And that's just what Harry needed him to do now.

"First thing is to find out exactly what they have on Nikki. This means that I go into the Sheriff's Office and dig around for the papers. I'll need you, Ollie, to keep O'Neil out of there just long enough for me to find the file and get out of there."

"Sure. How long do you need?"

"At least twenty minutes. Can you swing that?" Harry asked.

"No problem, Harry."

"Good. Now Little Bea will stick close to me."

"Why?" Little Bea whined. "Just 'cause I'm the smallest? Harry, that's not fair. I want a job like the rest of you."

"Bea, don't worry. You will have one of the most important jobs; I want you to keep me informed about what Rhoda is doing. Also, I need you to keep an eye on who comes in and out of the house. You can help me to keep the ladies on track."

"Okay," Little Bea said, brightened.

"Little Bea and I will also follow the professor. Keep an eye out for things that are odd, out of place. I still don't know about that one. He's too charming."

"Yeah, like a snake," Ollie piped up.

"But Harry...the professor's all the way in Miller's Cove."

Harry's gold eyes squinted just slightly, and they all watched as they turned from gold to green. Everyone knew that meant to back off. Harry wouldn't take any guff from anyone, even Little Bea. To her relief, Harry finally turned his attention to Ollie, again.

"Ollie, after we get the information from the Sheriff's Office, I want you to first go to the bakery and keep an eye on Roxey. I never did trust that one. While you're at it, watch the diner across the street. All of our suspects go there almost everyday. You can run by *The Twilight* at night, just to see what's happening."

"Oh boy! Who says there's no such thing as a free lunch?!"

Everyone laughed.

"Since our fastest member is Dewey, he will be the runner. I want you to keep everyone informed of updates. The rest of you, just stand by," Harry instructed. "Our guardians need our help. They can't go where we can or be inconspicuous, like us. We need to find out who did this horrible thing, and we need to find him soon. O'Neil is pressing to keep Nikki in jail."

Everybody made a tighter circle around Harry. Paws went in.

"Go, Cat Gang, go!"

****

Deputy Holloway was kind enough to go to Martha's and get Nikki a cheeseburger and a chocolate milkshake for dinner.

"How did you know?" Nikki was surprised that the deputy thought to bring anything in, let alone one of her favorite meals.

"Martha told me."

"Thank you so much."

"I'm sorry. I would stay, but I'm on patrol tonight. Officer Ryan will be here, if you need anything."

Smiling, Nikki said, "Okay. Thanks again for the dinner."

****

It was Saturday night. Heather was in bed and Harry sneaked out of the house. He walked to town with a purpose. He was on a mission: a mission of life or death. Nikki's, to be exact.

Little Bea wanted to tag along, but this was too dangerous for her. Ollie had more experience.

When Harry saw Ollie, he crossed the street.

"Did you have any trouble getting out?" Harry asked, knowing that Ollie's guardians were overprotective of him.

"Nope. I just spent the afternoon digging another hole under the fence."

The two cats proceeded in silence. Harry's plan to get into the Sheriff's Office was to have Ollie stand look out while Harry, using his power of teleportation, would get into the office and silently find Nikki's case file. From there, he'll see what they really have on Nikki.

Harry stopped in front of the Sheriff's Office.

"So, what's the plan?" Ollie asked.

"You just stay out here and be my lookout. If anyone comes near the place, yowl as loud as you can. All I need is twenty minutes."

"Sure, Harry. I can do that." Ollie hesitated. "But Harry...how do you know that O'Neil's not in there now?"

Harry sighed. His patience was running low and Ollie watched, as Harry's eyes changed from gold to green. Ollie knew he had asked the wrong question. He sat down in submission to Harry.

For a split second, Harry thought that maybe he should have gotten Dewey for this job. He's certainly brighter than Ollie. Well, too late to change now.

"Because," Harry said in a harsh tone, "Saturday night is O'Neil's poker night. There's no way he would miss out on that."

"Gosh. I forgot about the poker game, Harry. I guess that's why you're in charge, huh?"

Harry rolled his eyes. Ollie can't help being slow, but Harry gets tired of spelling things out for him.

"Okay. Once again. What are you going to do if *anyone* comes near this place?"

"Yowl as loud as I can."

"Good man."

With that, Harry was gone.

"I'll never get used to that," Ollie said to himself.

Inside, Harry walked along the desk tops until he found O'Neil's desk.

It figures it would be a mess, the man is such a pig, he thought with disgust.

Harry knew that he had told Ollie that he would only need twenty minutes, but it might take him more that twenty minutes to weed through this clutter, but he supposed that Ollie would stand guard for as long as Harry needed him to.

Harry began to look through all of the papers on the desk. If it didn't have Nikki's name on it, Harry slid it out of the way with his paw. By the time he found Nikki's paperwork, the floor was littered with forms, notes and files. Harry didn't pay attention to the mess he had created. He was focused on only one thing...Nikki's file.

By the time he finished reading all of the sheriff's notes on the case, he came to one conclusion...he was right. Sheriff had nothing on Nikki except the fact that she would inherit the family's money. Okay...that's enough motive for some people, but not for his Nikki. Then an idea struck him. He skimmed through all of the paperwork again.

Ah ha! Just as I thought. He isn't looking at anyone else for the murder. There were a lot of suspects. For instance, Professor Stu Walters. Lynn caught him with Miranda one night. He came up to the house the night before Lynn died, and started a huge fight. Then there was Rhoda. She was always jealous of Lynn and Stu and their relationship. Let's not forget Roxey, who needs money to get out of this town. Those were just three people he could name who have a motive and opportunity. More opportunity than Nikki, who lives in New York.

Harry's thoughts were broken by the sound of voices. He stopped and listened. It was the officer on duty, but who was he talking to, and *where was Ollie?* Oh well, no time to stop and wonder. Harry vanished in the blink of an eye and reappeared next to Ollie, who was preening himself.

"*Ollie!* What the heck happened to you?"

Ollie looked around and saw Harry and he was mad. "What? What happened?"

"Nothing, I almost got caught, that's all." Harry nudged Ollie up on his feet. "I was right about O'Neil." Harry began telling Ollie what he had found.

"I *knew* it!" exclaimed Ollie. "I knew that Nikki couldn't have done it!"

"Of course, she didn't. I knew that before I went in the office. What I wanted to know is what they think they have on her and who else are they looking into for the murder, the answer is they have nothing, but they're going to try to pin it on Nikki. Considering all of the good ol' boys on O'Neil's side, he'll do it, too. Unless we stop him."

"How are we going to do that?"

"Find the true killer, of course!"

Chapter 5

Sunday, December 9th

At 5:00 a.m. Heather awoke with a start. Her whole body ached from the tenseness related to all the stress she'd lived through the past few days. Finding that Lynn had died was bad enough, but then to have Nikki arrested on top of that...and for murder? It was unthinkable.

As she dragged herself out of bed, she wondered how they were treating Nikki. I hope they are feeding her well. *I'll take her some hot chocolate when I go visit her this afternoon.*

Harry was standing by Heather's door as if waiting for her to get up.

"Well, good morning, Harry. Looks like it's just you and me this morning, Bud."

"Trill," was Harry's answer.

He went to the Magic Cupboard and sat in front of it, turning to give Heather a soulful look.

"Okay, okay. I get the hint."

After feeding Harry, Heather put some coffee on and got some cereal and milk out. As she was eating her breakfast, she stared at the newspaper without reading the words. She was too preoccupied with this major mess that Nikki was in.

Heather cleared her breakfast dishes and went upstairs to shower and get dressed. She wandered into the office to get needed work done on her article. When the clock in the library struck 1:00 p.m., Heather grabbed her coat and gloves and ran out the door. She stopped by

Martha's to order a cocoa to take to Nikki and a sandwich for herself, which she quickly ate in the car before she headed to the jail.

****

Nikki was sitting on the hard rack they called a bed when Officer Ryan came by with breakfast from Martha's. She had gotten used to his grouchiness by now, so she didn't even try to start a conversation. At least the food was good.

Nikki counted herself lucky that Heather had brought her manuscript to work on. She filled her morning focused on writing, only taking a break when Officer Ryan brought her lunch.

Heather timed her visit perfectly, arriving soon after her last bite was finished.

"Hi. How are you? You need anything?" Heather handed Nikki the cup of cocoa from Martha's.

"Mmmm...thanks for the cocoa...you mean, besides getting the heck out of here? No."

"Tom called last night."

Nikki stopped blowing on her cocoa long enough to ask, "Why?"

"He said that he and his brother wanted to take us out to dinner."

"What did you tell him?"

"What could I tell him? The truth. That you were in jail on a trumped up charge of murdering your aunt."

A look of dread crossed Nikki's face, followed by resignation. "Oh, well. The whole town knows about it by now anyway. I'm surprised Tom didn't know about it last night."

"Nobody thinks that you actually killed Lynn."

Heather caught Nikki's look that clearly said, *yeah, right.*

"Well, no one that matters," said Heather.

"How's Harry doing?" Nikki inquired.

"He misses you just like I do. It's really heartbreaking how he sticks so close to me now...as if he's afraid of losing me, too."

"I miss you guys, too. I can't wait until I get out of here and take a real shower."

Heather smiled. "I'll bet. Okay, I'm going back to the house to try to finish my article. I wanted to get it done early for a change, but considering all that has happened, I'm probably going to turn it in at the last minute. Are you sure there isn't anything that I can get you?"

"No. Just take good care of Harry for me."

"I will. Don't worry. You'll be out of here before you know it."

The officer unlocked the cell door, and Heather left Nikki alone once more.

****

That evening, Greg came into the cell with a picnic basket full of roast beef, baked potatoes and fresh green salad with a choice of dressings.

"What's this?" Nikki said, wide-eyed.

"This," Deputy Holloway said with a sweeping gesture, "is dinner for two, courtesy of Martha."

He took a bottle of her favorite Zin and a corkscrew from the basket.

"Are you supposed to be drinking with a prisoner, officer?" Nikki said coquettishly.

"I'm off duty and besides, Ryan owes me a favor. And would you please call me by my given name?" He smiled and Nikki almost melted. *Hold on, girl!*

"Okay, Greg. How did you know that Zin was one of my favorite wines?'

His smile got wider. "Lucky guess."

They shared small talk over the delicious meal. Nikki was astonished at his treatment of her. He was gentle, kind, smart, witty and not too hard to look at, either.

Greg was pouring her a second glass of wine, when Nikki came back to the here and now.

"So, how long have you been here?"

"About two months."

"What brought you here?"

Greg's countenance changed at once. He put his glass on the floor and cleared his throat. "My wife died eight months ago of cancer."

Nikki suddenly felt her stomach tighten. "Gosh, I'm so sorry, Greg." *It's obvious that it was too soon to talk about it, it's too raw,* she thought.

"It's okay. People say that it'll get easier with time." Greg cleared his throat to fight against the tears. "Anyway, it was too hard to stay in Boston. I was in the Boston P.D. and was looking to transfer. My buddy, Robert, told me of a job opening up here and the rest is history."

After the bombshell that Greg had dropped on her, Nikki didn't know what to say. She felt uncomfortable; like she pried open wounds that were just healing.

"You look exhausted," Greg said, looking concerned.

Nikki suddenly felt guilty. *He's concerned about me, even after I just tromped all over his wife's memory.*

Greg started to pack the picnic basket with their used dishes.

"I'll let you get some rest. Tomorrow's the big day."

Nikki accepted Greg's hand and he helped her up. They stood so close, she could feel his breath on her skin. Nikki thought for sure that he heard her heart thumping. They stood like that for a moment more than they had to. It felt good to be close to a man again. *Too close. Back, girl!*

"Well, I'll see you tomorrow morning, Nikki."

Nikki smiled and nodded her head.

"Goodnight."

And he was gone.

Chapter 6

Monday, December 10th

Heather had spent half the night tossing and turning, and the other half drinking coffee and working on the article about the occult.

On Monday morning, Heather was anything but hungry, but she knew that she had to eat something. Besides the nervous feeling that she was experiencing, she had a stomach that burned with acid from the two pots of coffee she drank the night before. She slid some bread into the toaster oven and poured herself some orange juice instead of some more coffee.

Harry came in and mewed for his breakfast. "I didn't forget you." She poured some dry food in his dish and he raced over to gobble it down. Heather smiled.

Her mood grew sullen again. Heather could not believe it was only forty eight hours since they took Nikki away. The ding on the toaster sounded and she was soon nibbling on toast that tasted like cardboard. She ate about half and threw the rest away.

After taking her shower, Heather donned her jeans and a thick red cable knit sweater. She tore a hair brush through her thick, wavy, red mane. On automatic pilot, she went through the motions of brushing a little blush on her cheeks and darkened her red eyelashes with mascara, which brought out her bewitching aqua-blue eyes. She finished the transformation with a dab of wine colored lipstick.

"There." She stepped back to examine herself in the mirror. Disgusted with the outcome, she waved her hand toward her reflection.

Heather sat at the kitchen table as she drank the last of her orange juice, waiting anxiously for the courthouse to open. Mr. Wilson said that Nikki's case would be first on the docket. Finally, at 7:30, she couldn't wait any longer. She grabbed her keys and ran through the door.

Heather pulled into the courthouse parking lot at 7:45, fifteen minutes before they opened the doors for their first case of the day. She impatiently tapped her bright red fingernails on the steering wheel, watching the door for any signs of life. Finally, when she saw a woman unlock the door, Heather grabbed her purse and hurried inside.

Heather opened the door and was hit by a blast of warm air, making her aware of just how cold it was outside. Once she opened the heavy oak door, Heather felt as if she had walked into a different world. The walls were paneled with a rich, dark colored wood. Beginning at the third row from the back, there were rows of cushioned chairs where the spectators sat. Almost every chair was taken with the town's gawkers, including Rhoda of course. *I didn't think that this town had so many people.*

Heather sat as close to the railing (that divided the lawyers, plaintiff and defendants from the citizens) as she could get. When she looked up, she noticed Nikki coming through a side door with someone in a uniform that Heather had never seen before. Nikki was scanning the spectator's area until her eyes landed on Heather, who gave her a reassuring smile. Nikki's face betrayed the stress that she had been going through over the last four days, when they had first arrived in Harrot Reef and found Lynn's body.

Heather mouthed, "It's okay."

Nikki gave Heather a weak smile in response.

"All rise."

The judge entered and immediately Heather knew that Nikki was in trouble. He looked at Nikki and scowled. He held Nikki's gaze as he sat down.

"Please be seated."

There was a rustling from people sitting down and making themselves comfortable for the show that was about to begin.

After a brief discussion with the prosecutor and Mr. Wilson, the judge set a million dollar bail. It seems that everyone in the courtroom gasped with surprise. The judge slammed down the gavel and bellowed, "Court is adjourned!" It was all over before Heather knew it.

Heather had to keep herself from standing up and telling the "court" where he could stick his million dollar bail! Everyone knew Nikki couldn't hurt, let alone kill, *and* why such a high bail? Surely they know that she isn't a flight risk. Clearly the judge is in O'Neil's pocket. Speaking of O'Neil, Heather looked across the aisle and saw him grinning from ear to ear. *He's sooo pleased with himself.*

The courtroom started to empty. Nikki stood and turned to her friend and Heather saw the concern wash over her face.

Heather put her hand up. "Don't worry. I'll put up my condo."

Nikki started to argue.

Heather held up her hand. "No. It's all set. Besides, you're not going to skip town, right?" She smiled as she watched Nikki through the side door.

****

Heather pushed her way through the door to the sheriff's department to find Deputy Holloway sitting at the reception desk. She hurried up to him.

"How is she?"

"She's fine, Heather."

"I've paid her bail at the courthouse. They told me to come over here to get her."

"Would you mind filling these forms out, while I get Nikki."

Taking up the pen, she raised her eyebrow when he turned to go. "It's Nikki now, eh?" she whispered to herself. As she was signing the first form, she felt the cold air on her back. She turned to find Tom scurrying to the desk.

"What are you doing here?"

Heather was surprised by his accusatory tone. "Getting Nikki out."

"That's why I'm here."

Nikki came out just in time to hear this exchange. "Thank you both. I couldn't spend one more minute in there."

"Rotten trick to arrest you on a Saturday when they knew you wouldn't get a bail hearing until Monday." Heather glared at Deputy Holloway.

Holloway held his hands up in surrender. "Hey. I didn't have anything to do with it."

"You were there, weren't you?" Heather was getting her Irish up.

"Just doing my job. For your information, I never thought Nikki had anything to do with her aunt's death."

Just then the sheriff came in with the freezing wind.

"What are all these people doing here?"

"They are here to bail Miss Johnson out," the deputy answered.

"Have they filled out the paperwork?"

"Yes, sir."

"Then get them out of here," O'Neil yelled over his shoulder as he went into the inner office.

Nikki, Heather and Tom all shivered in the cold. Nikki thanked Tom again for coming to help, slipped the hood of her jacket over her head and followed Heather to the car.

"Tom asked me what I was doing there, like I wasn't supposed to help you out. I guess he wanted to be the big hero," Heather said as she pulled the car door shut.

"Don't take it personally. That's just Tom. You remember that I told you we went out for a while in high school. I really wasn't ready for a commitment so we opted to be friends...close friends. He's just overprotective of me, that's all."

"Hmm. Are you sure that he knows that you are just *friends?*"

"Heather, don't be ridiculous! Of course he knows we're just friends."

"Okay. I'm just saying..." Changing the subject, Heather asked, "Did you eat anything today? Do you want to stop at Martha's?"

"No, I just want to go home and take a long, hot shower."

Heather smiled. "Of course. Did they feed you?"

"Oh, yeah. Greg went out and got me meals everyday."

"Greg? "

"Deputy Holloway." Nikki blushed.

"Oh, so now it's Greg, eh?"

"Heather, he's very nice. He treated me very well and he really didn't think that I did it."

They pulled up in front of house.

"Just be careful, girl."

Chapter 7

Tuesday, December 11th

The next morning, Nikki suggested that they go to Martha's for breakfast.

As Nikki and Heather got out of the car, it started to snow. They raced into Martha's and at once felt the warmth of the small diner. The place was empty; even the locals weren't in.

"Where is everybody, Martha?"

"I don't know. None of my regulars came in today. I guess it's the weather. You know there's a storm brewing and they are saying there will be a blizzard before nightfall. So, how are you?" She looked at Nikki with concern.

"Okay. The deputy treated me well. He brought me some food from here."

"I know," she smiled. "He's a nice boy."

"He's hardly a boy, Martha," Nikki retorted.

"Okay okay! What'd you guys want to eat?"

"I think I want bacon and eggs and hash browns, eggs over easy, and some coffee, please."

She turned to Heather, ready with pen and pad and asked, "And what can I get you?"

Heather nodded. "I'll have the same, please."

After Martha walked away, Heather asked Nikki, "So what about Greg?"

"What about Greg?"

"Well?"

"He's just a nice guy. He treated me really well when I was there."

"Hmm. I see."

"Really Heather, he is very nice."

"Yeah you told me that."

Deputy Greg Holloway came through the door and saw Nikki and Heather. He grinned impishly and casually strolled to their table.

"Well, I see you got your breakfast." He winked at Nikki. "May I join you ladies?"

Nikki blushed as Heather gave her a knowing smile. Heather scooted over and patted the bench beside her.

"Sure."

Greg hesitated, looking first at Heather and then at Nikki, who shrugged nonchalantly. At the very sight of him, Nikki's stomach filled with butterflies and she felt like a silly schoolgirl.

When he sat down next to her, their eyes met. Just for a moment, but that was enough. Nikki looked away, but she still felt his hazel eyes on her.

Heather was amused. She cleared her throat, bringing the thoughts of the other two back to the table.

"So, I hear that you took care of our friend. I mean, bringing her food and everything."

Holloway looked at her with a smile. "Well, I couldn't let her go hungry, now could I?"

Martha returned to their table quickly, putting a cup of steamy, hot coffee on the table for Greg. "What would you like, breakfast or lunch?"

"Oh, I think I'll have breakfast. Eggs, sausage, biscuits and some of your delicious homemade gravy, please," Greg said without looking at a menu.

"Coming up."

Greg turned his attention back to Nikki and Heather. "So, now what are you gals going to do today?"

"Find out who killed my aunt," Nikki snapped.

"Nikki, leave that to us. We wouldn't want you to get hurt," he warned.

Shaking her head vigorously, Nikki said, "There is no way that O'Neil will cut me a break. He has it out for my family. No, if I want to clear myself, I'll have to do it on my own."

Heather chimed in, "With my help, as well."

"Okay, okay." Greg held his hands up in surrender. "At least let me help."

Nikki looked at him skeptically. She hesitated, "No. We don't need your help."

"It may help if he is on the inside. Maybe..." Heather looked hopefully at Greg, "he can get us information that we would otherwise not have. He knows the inside track."

"But who says that he will share it. No. My mind is made up. We will prove that I didn't do it and find out who did...and we will do it alone."

Greg shrugged. "Okay. If that's the way you want it. It's just that these people are more likely to open up to me, rather than you." He pulled out his badge. "But if you want to go at it alone, be my guest."

He dug into one of the biscuits and scooped up some of the gravy and shoved it in his mouth. Turning toward the counter where Martha was prepping silverware, he caught her eye.

"Martha, this is great gravy!"

Martha grinned. "Of course! What did you expect?"

The door blew open bringing a handsome young man into the little diner. He brushed the snow off of his coat and ran his fingers through his thick, red curls making sure that all of the snow was out.

"Hey, Robert. Over here," Greg hollered.

Robert turned around and waved at Greg. He sauntered over to the table with a manner that showed both confidence and cockiness, and sat down next to Heather.

"So what's going on?"

Robert made no attempt to hide the fact that he was practically leering at Heather. He smiled a crooked sexy smile, which was probably the only thing that wasn't perfect about him. His gorgeous blue eyes seemed to sparkle.

Greg cleared his throat and Robert tore his eyes away from Heather and acknowledged the rest of the group.

"Nikki, Heather, this is my oldest and best friend, Robert Hayes. He's the one who convinced me to leave the big city and come to Harrot Reef. Robert is also the nurse who took care of your aunt, Nikki."

Immediately, Nikki's hackles were raised. *So this is the jerk who left Aunt Lynn when she was so sick.*

"Robert, this is Nikki Johnson and her friend Heather...er"

"Murphy. Heather Murphy."

"Well, hi Heather Murphy." Robert took her hand and held it a little longer than was necessary, then turned his eyes toward Nikki.

"Nikki," he said curtly. He shook her hand across the table.

"So, is anyone going to tell me what's going on?"

"Did you know that Lynn Johnson died on Thursday?"

Robert nodded his head. "I heard. I just came into town and stopped for some gas. Billy Green told me. Lynn told me to go ahead and see my family and that she would be okay. If I would have known...'""

"Well, Nikki is her niece. She came up here to spend Christmas with Lynn and found her dead."

"Oh no...really...how terrible! Are you alright?" Robert seemed sincere.

Nikki nodded her head. Something about this guy. For some reason, she couldn't pinpoint why, she felt an instant distrust for him. Before she could dwell on it further, her thoughts were interrupted when she heard Greg explaining the situation.

"So, O'Neil is giving her a hard time just because she was first on the scene," Greg continued.

"I heard that she died in the library," Robert said.

Nikki's answer was barely above a whisper. "Yes, that's right."

"Well, she could have died from a heart attack," Robert suggested. "Her blood pressure was high."

"Not likely." Nikki cleared her thoughts away. "Granted, Aunt Lynn's blood pressure was a tad bit high, but she took care of it with diet and essential oils. she even drank some kind of special tea to control it. She always thought that any kind of medicine was poison to the body. Her medicine cabinet was filled with oils for any affliction and she had a whole cabinet in the kitchen jamb packed with teas, herbs etc. Anyway, her health was excellent. She ran five miles a day. She was a phenomenal lady."

Greg smiled. "Agreed. She was always so nice to me. I remember last year, when I had bronchitis, she brought me homemade chicken soup. I swear that soup was the reason why I got well!"

Robert said to Nikki, "Lynn was my favorite patient. Honestly Nikki, I wouldn't have left if I Lynn hadn't insisted that I go visit my family. She said that she would be fine with Rhoda coming in a couple times a day."

Robert seemed sincere, but Nikki was having trouble buying it. If he was a professional nurse, why didn't he stay until Aunt Lynn was well? Was it because he wanted to give himself an alibi?

Heather felt the tension exuding from Nikki. *Time to change the subject.* "Well, what is our first move?" Heather leaned forward in her seat, waiting for Greg to take the lead.

"Well, first off, you need to find the receipt from Rick's Place."

"Why? What would that prove?" Nikki inquired.

"Well, the toxicology report hasn't come in yet, but if it shows something like a slow acting poison you more than likely would be in the clear."

Nikki and Heather grabbed their purses and rifled through them again in search of something that would prove that, at the time Lynn died, they were miles away. They both came up empty.

"I normally get rid of them right after I log them into my phone. Hey! My phone! I usually log them into my phone." Heather started to look for her cellphone in her bag.

"No. That won't work," Greg said.

Nikki, with her hand still in the purse, looked up at Greg quizzically.

"It has to be a hard copy receipt because the time of service is on it."

Nikki's expression changed from hopeful to anguished in a flash. "So, we are back where we started."

"Not necessarily. I have an idea." Greg brightened.

"Yeah? What?" Nikki countered.

"You want to have dinner out tonight?" Greg asked.

"That's your idea? To have dinner out? Tonight? How will that help?"

Greg answered Nikki, "Let's go to…what's that restaurant?"

"You mean Rick's Place? Yeah, what about it?"

"I'll get a warrant for your receipt. Wait. How did you did pay?"

"Credit card." Nikki found herself sitting on the edge of her seat, heart pounding and hopeful again. "Greg, what do you have in mind?"

"Well, I suggest that we go to Rick's Place with a warrant, get a copy of your receipt. It should show the time. That way we can and show it to O'Neil. It'll get you out off of his radar."

"And if it doesn't have the time stamped?" Nikki asked skeptically.

"We will cross that bridge if and when we come to it."

Greg touched Nikki's arm and looked into at her with those soft hazel eyes. She felt like a weight had been lifted from her shoulders. She almost smiled at Greg and nodded her head.

"Things will be alright, Nikki. I believe you. We just have to find the guy who did this."

Robert surprised her when he agreed. He didn't even know her. Maybe Aunt Lynn told him about her. She still didn't quite trust him.

The door swung open again, and the tinkle of the bell above the door sounded Tom's arrival. He looked around the restaurant and his eyes settled on Nikki.

"Hi guys. Can I join you?"

Tom was dragging the chairs over to the table without waiting for an answer.

Greg showed his annoyance. He said in a very low voice, "Yeah, go right ahead and butt in."

When Greg saw that Nikki was giggling behind her hand, he blushed and then smiled that golden smile in her direction.

"So what's the subject?" Tom asked.

"We were just talking about Lynn's murder. O'Neil still thinks that Nikki is guilty," Heather answered.

Tom leaned forward and grabbed Nikki's hand and Greg could barely hide his disdain. "So, what are we going to do about it?" Tom glanced at Greg and seemed to whither under his look.

"We're just formulating our plan now." Greg reached under the table and laid his hand on Nikki's knee.

The mood changed when Sheriff O'Neil strutted in. He scanned the restaurant and when he saw his deputy at the same table as his number one suspect, he bellowed at him, "What are you doing here with … her? Don't you have anything better to do, like trying to find proof for our case? You shouldn't be here with our only suspect."

Greg swallowed his last bite of biscuit. "I was hungry so I came in to eat, and I saw these beautiful ladies sitting here all by themselves. So I joined them. It's not against the law, is it?"

"No, but it's unethical and I don't like it. They don't need to know about our case. Especially since one of them is a suspect," he repeated stronger this time. He glared at Greg, and then looked at Nikki as if she was a piece a fish that had been sitting out for a week.

O'Neil turned red with anger, but before he could say anything else, Heather jumped in. "Sheriff, he didn't say anything about the *"case"* and we didn't ask. We were just sitting enjoying breakfast."

The sheriff grumbled and turned to walk away. He stopped and said over his shoulder, "Holloway, get back to work."

Greg waited until Grady O'Neil left with his coffee, then rolled his eyes.

"How can you stand him? I don't even know him and I can tell he's a jerk." Heather's face showed her disgust.

"Yeah, well, mostly I just let everything that he says go in one ear and out the other." Greg grabbed his check and reached for Nikki's and Heather's, as well.

"That's alright. We will pay our own way. You paid for my food all weekend," Nikki said..

"Thanks anyway," Heather said.

Greg dropped the check where it was. Getting up, he bowed his head slightly, "Ladies," and left the restaurant.

Robert followed Greg out of the restaurant.

Tom sat quietly, listening to Nikki and Heather talk.

"I thought you said that Greg was nice," Heather confronted Nikki.

Nikki squirmed uncomfortably. "He is."

"So, why wouldn't you accept his help?"

Nikki avoided Heather's eyes. Tom leaned forward listening intently.

"He only wants to help," Heather stated.

"I know. It's just that I don't know who I can trust. I only met Greg a few nights ago. What if he is playing 'good cop' to O'Neil's 'bad cop'?"

"Well, I say take a chance and let him in..."

Tom spoke up. "But proceed with caution."

They finished their coffee in silence, each in their own thoughts. Martha approached. "Do you guys want more coffee?"

Tom held up his cup, and Martha poured the dark, steamy liquid.

Heather and Nikki grabbed their things and scooted out of the booths.

"No, thanks," they said in unison.

"Thanks for the, as always, yummy breakfast." Nikki said to Martha, gave her a peck on the cheek and followed Heather out of the diner.

****

When they pulled up in front of the house, the wind began to blow, and the snow that was falling gently five minutes earlier, had now started to whip around the car. The sky was dark with clouds and it felt later than 12:30.

Nikki put the car in park and turned off the engine. "We haven't even unpacked the things we brought yet. I only brought enough for the stay. I still have the reading of the will to go to. We'll have to go and shop for clothes until O'Neil says we can leave."

"Yeah. You can't leave the area, and that sounds more practical than me having to drive to NYC to pick up our clothes and things, and then back all this way," Heather answered.

They got out of the car and slowly walked up the steps, backs hunched against the wind. Their hoods were up, covering their faces, as well as their heads. Even though the weather had turned blustery and gloomy, thinking of the future lightened the mood considerably. Nikki unlocked the door paned with stained glass, opened it and almost stepped on Harry's tail.

"Harry! Why do you always have to lie down right in front of the door?"

"Trill."

Heather raised her voice so that Nikki could hear. "Robert seems like a nice guy. It was sure nice to meet the nurse who took care of Lynn, don't you think, Nikki?"

Nikki threw her keys on the kitchen table, took off her coat and scarf.

"Hey. Nikki? What's the matter? Don't you like Robert?"

Nikki turned to look at her friend. "I never said that, it's just that..."

"What? What's wrong with him? He seemed genuinely concerned."

Nikki plopped down on a chair and traced her fingernail along the table. She was thinking about the best way to broach the subject.

"Nikki?"

"Okay. I know that on the whole he appears to want whoever is doing this to be stopped, but I don't know. I just get the feeling that there is something else. I feel that he might have his own agenda and it has nothing to to with proving I'm not guilty or finding the real murderer."

"You sound paranoid now. Robert is Greg's best friend. He wouldn't have brought Robert in on this if he couldn't be trusted. You need to stop thinking everyone is out to get you, Nikki. You can trust some people, you know?"

"Trust people? It's hard to trust people when you have no idea who is trustworthy. I don't know a lot of people in town anymore since I haven't been here in about six months and I usually only stay about two weeks at a time. I certainly don't know why anyone would kill Aunt Lynn. It has to be something that she told somebody... something that she had that was either worth money or that threatened someone in town."

"Do you think that she had some information that got her killed? No. That only happens on TV. I'd say that she had something that someone wanted. Or that somebody thought she had...maybe the Pink Diamond?"

"Oh, that's just silly, Heather. It's just a story...like a fairytale...that people in our family used to tell. There's nothing to it."

"How do you know? Maybe your Uncle Frank did come back with it. Maybe he did hide it for some reason. Maybe he knew that someone was after it. You did say it was priceless, didn't you?"

Nikki nodded her head slowly and added, "That's what the *story* says." There was a moment of silence between them, then Nikki jumped up from her seat, grabbed the coffee pot and poured herself some coffee left over from this morning. She held the pot up, as if to ask if Heather wanted some.

Heather shook her head. She had too much coffee already and her stomach was telling her as much. Between the coffee and the stress of the situation, Heather doubted that she would ever drink coffee again...at least, not this time.

When Nikki got her coffee out of the microwave, she went back to her seat at the kitchen table. She blew on the hot liquid and squinted her eyes as she took a sip.

"I don't trust Robert," Nikki flatly stated.

Heather opened her mouth to argue the point, but Nikki raised her hand to stop her.

"Oh, I know he's charming. It's just this feeling I get about him. I mean, he left Aunt Lynn when she was sick!"

Heather came to Robert's defense. "He only left because Lynn told him to. You heard him."

"Yeah, I know, but who's to say that he isn't lying? Did anybody actually hear my aunt tell him to go? I don't know, Heather, I just don't trust him."

"Robert is a friend of Greg's. If he trusts him, surely you can, too. Since he was your aunt's nurse, he has an interest in this, too. He wants to help, Nikki. If he didn't want to, I would think you'd be more suspicious." Heather stood and got the cocoa down from the cupboard.

Nikki shook her head. She fell silent, feeling the anxiety growing in the pit of her stomach. Petting Harry seemed to have a calming effect. *Okay. Maybe now is the time to drop my misgivings toward Robert...for now.*

Chapter 8

Wednesday, December 12th

The next morning Heather and Nikki stayed home and rearranged the furniture.

In the afternoon, Heather decided to do some more research on her article. The house was quiet...almost too quiet. Nikki looked out at the snow falling softly on the ground.

While Heather was doing research, delving into the minds of those who practice witchcraft, Nikki was making phone calls to set up everything for the memorial. The last call she made was to the florist, who guided her through what she would need. She crossed off the last of the tasks that she had to do. Nikki sighed. *That's all done.*

It was then that her phone rang. Nikki didn't want to talk to anybody. She was spent, worn to a frazzle. She had spent the last hours trying to make all of the arrangements for the ceremony. The last thing that she wanted to do was to talk anymore on the phone. What if it was the creep that had been bothering her.

Nikki reluctantly answered her cellphone. "Hello?"

"Hi, Nikki?"

"Yes."

"This is Jonathan Wilson, your aunt's attorney."

"Yes, Mr. Wilson. What can I do for you?"

"Well first off, how are you holding up?" he asked.

"I'm okay," Nikki said, knowing that she was lying through her teeth. She was anything but okay, and she wished that people would stop asking her that inane question.

"Good," was his absent-minded response. "I want to make an appointment for you to come down here for the reading of your Aunt Lynn's will. Will tomorrow at 10:00 a.m. work for you?"

"That would be fine."

"Good. I'll see you then."

Heather walked into the room as Nikki was hanging up the phone.

"Who was that?"

Nikki crossed the room, sat down on the couch and scooped Harry up into her arms.

"Mr. Wilson. He wants me to come down to his office for the reading of Aunt Lynn's will."

"Oh, good. What time?"

"10:00 a.m....will you go with me?"

Heather looked across the room at her friend. She looked so vulnerable right then. How could she say no?

"Of course I will."

They spent a few minutes planning the dinner menu. It was decided that they would melt butter in a glass dish and throw some chicken thighs in with a cup of sherry. Stick it in the oven, and voila, it was done. It was quick and easy.

Heather stood and stretched. "I'm going back to work on my article. You okay?"

Nikki nodded her head. "Yes," she sighed. "I'm okay. How is it going? The article, I mean."

"Well. It's not easy to write about things you know nothing about, as you know, but it's coming along. Thank goodness there is a lot of material out there on witchcraft. So...what are you going to do?"

"I think I'll start the chicken for dinner, then work on my manuscript until it's done."

"Have you broken through that block that you had? Heather asked.

"Oh, yes. I created another character that brought more depth to the story. Funny thing, I brought this character in the story when I was in jail."

Heather was intrigued. "Who is this character. I mean, did you base him or her on anyone?"

Nikki smiled, looking off in the distance. "Yeah. Sheriff O'Neil."

They both broke into laughter.

Chapter 9

Thursday, December 13th

At 10:00 a.m the next morning, Heather and Nikki were seated comfortably in Mr. Wilson's office. It was roomy and had a very warm atmosphere. The walls were covered with a rich, dark paneling, enhanced with lovely paintings by local artists. To the right of the doorway stood a blue velour couch and matching wing chairs forming a cozy area for meetings. This is where the three of them gathered.

"Nikki. It's so good to see you. Are you still having trouble sleeping?"

Obviously, Nikki's dark circles were showing through the fair foundation used in an unsuccessful attempt to cover them. Yes, she had trouble sleeping. Who wouldn't? The last remaining member of her family, besides herself, was gone; and not just gone, but killed. A murder for which the sheriff wanted her to take the blame. Nikki found herself close to tears...again. *No. I will not let go here!*

Nikki looked at her hands in her laps that were clutching a tissue. She slowly nodded her head.

"Well, let's proceed quickly so that you can get on with your day." Mr. Wilson opened Lynn Johnson's file. He cleared his throat before going on. "As expected, your aunt left everything to you; the home, one hundred million dollars in stocks, bonds, etc."

"*What?* You're kidding! I knew there was money in the family, but I really had no idea that it was that much." Nikki leaned forward to try to read the will.

Heather gasped. "Gosh, Nikki. You mean you didn't know? Why didn't your family tell you?"

"I don't know. I guess Mom and Dad must've known, but I was too young to understand so they clearly never had a chance to tell me that before they died. Maybe Aunt Lynn figured there would be enough time to discuss my inheritance later."

Mr. Wilson cleared his throat to get Nikki's attention again. "There is one contingency."

"What's that?" Nikki inquired.

The lawyer looked up. "You need to keep Harry at the family home. Otherwise you give up your entire inheritance."

"Well, I would never get rid of Harry anyway, so there's no problem there." *I know that Harry has to be older than he seems, since he has always been there for me as long as I can remember, so I wouldn't abandon him in his old age. I wouldn't think of giving Harry away. I couldn't imagine life without him.*

"Here is the key to a safe deposit box that your aunt had." Mr. Wilson handed her an envelope.

As if in a daze, Nikki took the envelope. All that money!

Nikki snapped out of her confusion when Heather softly said her name. She turned to find her friend standing at the opened door. Heather motioned for her to go.

They drove home in quiet contemplation. Heather decided it would be better for Nikki to let all that just happened soak in.

It wasn't until they were home that Heather finally broke the silence. "Well, that was strange."

"What?"

Nikki walked into the kitchen and began to make a pot of coffee.

"That your aunt didn't tell you about the money."

Nikki turned to Heather, "She must've thought there was more time. She wasn't very old, you know. She probably didn't think about it."

Heather shrugged. "I guess so."

Harry sauntered into the room, sat in front of the Magic Cupboard, looked at Nikki and meowed loudly.

Heather laughed. "Dinner time."

Nikki smiled and filled Harry's dish.

Suddenly, Nikki blurted out, "I don't know if I want to live all by myself in this big house. What would you think about moving in with me? We both could do our work from here. I can work on my novel. There's more than enough space." Nikki gazed around her. "Besides, there is something special about this house that draws me to it. So, what do you say? You in?"

Heather had to take only a minute before saying, "I think it would be practical. I mean, why pay mortgages for two condominiums when we can share a big house."

"It would have higher maintenance, but we can make that work, considering the inheritance."

Heather felt her excitement building. "Okay! We'll have to wait until this mess is over and we can go back to New York and get ready to put the condos on the market."

They made their plans over a cup of coffee. Harry was on Nikki's lap, purring noisily, as if to confirm that everything was as it should be.

****

Half an hour later found them upstairs in their rooms unpacking the few things that they brought with them. They had planned on visiting no more than a week or two there at the most...time to make sure Aunt Lynn was well again. That was before Aunt Lynn's murder.

Nikki surprised herself when she heard humming and realized that it was coming from her own body. She turned, folding her favorite bulky sweater to put it away. From out of the blue, as if materializing magically, she saw that Harry was sitting on top of the dresser, looking down into the open drawer. She looked at him and smiled.

"Now, where did you come from, you little sneak?"

Harry picked up his head and looked at Nikki with golden eyes that bore right through to her very soul. She shivered, even though there was a roaring fire in the fireplace. She reached out to pet him. It was strange how, in a matter of days, things change. Nikki's smile faded as she thought about her favorite aunt and how she had looked just a week ago. Harry seemed to hear her thoughts and trilled softly at her. She dropped the sweater in the drawer, picked him up and went to sit in front of the fire.

As soon as Nikki carried Harry to the fireplace to sit, Harry squirmed out of her arms and trotted over to the dresser again. He jumped into the open drawer and began digging through the sweaters.

"Oh no you don't! Harry, get down!"

Nikki scooped Harry up and out of the drawer in one fast movement. She gently dropped him on the ground and tapped his hind end lightly. Harry turned and jumped on top of the clothing again.

"What is it, Harry?"

Nikki watched as Harry started to paw through the newly folded clothes. When she reached in and started to move the sweaters aside Harry sat back on his haunches.

"What is it that you want, Harry?"

"Trill," was Harry's response.

Nikki emptied the drawer and found a small envelope. She brought it over to the chair and opened it. Inside was a torn piece of note paper with numbers on it.

"15R, 32L, 5R. Hmm, I wonder what this could be."

"Trill," Harry answered.

****

Heather stopped at the threshold of the room where she'd been staying. It had a sitting area a couch in front of a fireplace, like Nikki's, only it was decorated in royal blue. The fireplace had a white marble mantle that was intricately carved. The drapes were made of royal blue velvet, which could be tied back to show white sheers. The bed was a four-poster, with an elegant royal blue velvet bedspread to match the drapes. The dresser and make-up table were made from cherry wood polished to a high sheen. The room had beautiful hardwood floors, with two luxurious Persian rugs. Standing there, taking in the opulence of the suite, Heather could hardly believe that she would be living so extravagantly on a full time basis.

Heather walked over to her suitcase that was left open on the chair in front of the fireplace. She hated living out of a suitcase, but she was too busy to be bothered to take the time to unpack until now. Heather picked up her angora sweater that she wore on the first day. Was it only four days ago? It seemed like a lifetime ago.

Heather's reflections were broken by a noise. She stood still and heard the sweet, melodic humming coming from Nikki's room, down the hall. A few minutes ago, when Heather left her, Nikki was so sad that Heather wondered when she might smile again, let alone hum pleasantly like this. Nikki continued with the nameless tune like she hadn't a care in the world. Heather's thoughts immediately jumped from how horrible the past four days were, to almost unimaginable possibilities flowing through her mind like a waterfall.

Nikki had said that she regularly brought pu-erh tea up when she visited. What if it *was* Nikki who laced it with extra arsenic? Nikki knew that Lynn drank it everyday, so it wouldn't take much. She could poison Lynn slowly, methodically. She even has an alibi, the best one that Heather could think of…Nikki wasn't here when Lynn died. What's to keep her from doing the simple calculations. The container says that it holds enough for thirty cups. Nikki knew that her aunt drank one cup a day for her blood pressure. All Nikki would have to do is to add more arsenic and count the days back from when she planned to come visit, and give Lynn the tea then. She could even have used me as a witness.

Wait a minute, Heather. This is Nikki we're talking about. Heather shook her head and started to fold the sweater that she was clutching in her hands a little too tightly. Then she stopped again. "But, still…"

Heather's thoughts were shattered when she heard Nikki.

"I'm hungry and we didn't get anything for dinner. What do you want to do, go to the store and get something to cook or do you want to go out to eat somewhere? There's a place on harbor way called Twilight Tavern. We can go and have lobster and afterward, stop at the lounge. They have the best hot buttered rum in Maine."

Heather swept her dark thoughts from her mind. "I'm in!"

****

By the time Nikki and Heather reached the restaurant the weather had changed. the wind had picked up and the dark sky was threatening to snow again. They rushed into the two-story building and were immediately enveloped by warm air.

The first floor showcased a lounge, where people were gathered by two fireplaces, one on each side of the long room. There were conversation pits with comfortable plush chairs and loveseats scattered here and there. On the far side of the room was a beautiful antique oak bar, polished to a high gloss.

They grabbed a table next to one of the fireplaces and shed the outer layers of jackets, scarves and gloves. Nikki rubbed her hands over her arms shivering as she did so. When the waitress came, they both ordered a glass of wine.

When it came, Nikki took a sip before saying, "I'm feeling kind of numb. Like the whole thing is just some kind of nightmare. I feel so many different emotions. Of course, I feel sad for Aunt Lynn, but then I feel anger toward the killer and I'm afraid that I will end up in jail. I want to find out who murdered Aunt Lynn for justice for both of us. Is that selfish?"

"I don't think so. Anyone would worry about being convicted of murder. Nikki, let's be real. Do you think Lynn would want you to mourn for her? From what you said, she wasn't that kind of person. You need to concentrate on proving your innocence, for Lynn as well as yourself."

Nikki nodded her head. "I guess you are right. Anyway, I have no idea where to start. Someone in this town knows what happened, and I've got to find that person. I don't know how long I'll have before…," her voice trailed off.

They fell into silence and became animated only when they heard their table was ready. Walking upstairs, you could feel an immediate change in atmosphere.

While the lounge was casual, the restaurant was a picture of elegance. It was done in a light-colored wood. The room was lit by recessed lighting. A wooden lattice hung from the ceiling by heavy several chains, with vines that intertwined through the structure. This piece of art was accented by recessed lighting that shone through the lattice down to the polished tables below. It was an original design that was made by a local woodcraft artist.

They were led to one of the tables overlooking the harbor. Heather couldn't help but notice the subdued tones of the restaurant. She looked at the menu, and was overwhelmed by the number of choices offered. Nikki leaned over. In a hushed tone she said, "Try the Lobster Thermidor. They are known for it here."

After ordering two lobster thermidors and two more glasses of wine to go with dinner, Heather looked around and was obviously impressed. "This is a really nice place for a small town like this."

"Yeah. I never realize how much I miss being here until I come and visit Aunt Lynn."

"The town is so...quaint. It's like something out of a painting."

"I know. Half of the buildings are from the 1800s. Of course, some were rebuilt, but the foundations are the originals," Nikki said.

Out of habit, Heather looked in her purse for her cell to check messages and couldn't find it. Panic started to fill her mind.

"Heather, what's the matter?"

"Nikki, didn't I have my phone earlier?"

"I think you had it downstairs. Yeah, I remember now. You had pulled it out and put it on the table. Why? Don't you have it?"

"No!" Heather started to tear at the things in her purse, but didn't find the phone.

"I'll go look for it downstairs, if you want."

"No, you wait here. I'll be right back."

Heather came back to the table a few minutes later with relief written all over her face. "Found it!"

Heather looked out the window and exclaimed, "Oh my gosh! Would you look at that? It's starting to snow again."

"Maybe it'll stop by the time we are ready to go home."

"I hope so. Just the thought of walking down the block to the parking lot makes me cold." Heather shivered.

They ate, drank wine and talked through the dinner about moving into the manor. Heather was careful not to talk about Aunt Lynn death, which so obviously was bothering Nikki. *She'll share more with me in her own time.*

When they were through, the waitress came around to offer dessert. They ordered chocolate mousse and espresso, then watched the snow gently falling as they relaxed for the first time in, what seemed to Nikki, to be much longer than it had actually had been. After dinner, they returned to the lounge for a hot buttered rum. By the time that they left, it had stopped snowing for the moment. They hurried to the car and climbed the hill to the Harrot Reef Manor.

Chapter 10

Friday, December 14th

Friday afternoon, Nikki was lost in thought when the doorbell rang. Nikki panicked. She just knew in her heart that it was the sheriff coming to haul her off again. Heather patted her hand before leaving the kitchen to see who it was. It was not until Heather came back into the room leading a woman, that Nikki became aware she'd been holding her breath. She let it out slowly and approached the woman.

"Hi. I'm Rhoda from down the street." The woman didn't look a day over 40, but Nikki knew from Aunt Lynn's description of her, she was in her late 50s. She was petite and in great shape for her years. Her grey hair was cut into a bob. She had striking blue eyes, but they made you feel as though she was stripping you clean of your walls that hid all of your secrets. Her smile came too easily and was as phony as a two dollar bill.

Nikki found her voice. "Oh, yes. She talks…talked about you a lot." *She told me what a gossiping busybody you are, and she didn't trust you as far she could throw you.* "It's so good to able to match the face with the name," trying hard to keep the sarcasm from brimming into her words.

Heather, seeing that trouble was brewing in her friend, quickly changed the subject. "We bought some delicious eclairs from the bakery. Would you like one with a cup of coffee?"

"That would be nice," Rhoda said, nodding her head.

When Nikki turned toward the kitchen, Heather jumped in. "Nikki, sit with our guest. I'll get it."

After they sat in the living room, Rhoda said, "I'm so sorry about your aunt." Her words sounded as if she truly meant it, but her eyes betrayed her. "We were so close. Whenever one was in need, the other was always there. I'm really going to miss her."

Nikki thought about all of the times that Aunt Lynn told her that Rhoda was a pain, always complaining about everybody in the town. Aunt Lynn was sure that she complained about her to others, as well.

One story really stuck in Nikki's mind about when Aunt Lynn and Stu, Rhoda's love interest, got together.

Stu Waters was a professor at the University of New England. He had it all; money, brains and good looks. With his full head of grey hair and salt and pepper beard, he looked distinguished and handsome. His intelligent hazel eyes seemed to look right through you. He wore stylish clothes that fit his tall, lanky body as if they were custom made. He was as charming as the day is long. All in all, he could take a woman's breath away...and Rhoda was obsessed with him.

Aunt Lynn had shared with Nikki that when Rhoda first told her about Stu, her eyes lit up and her otherwise pallid face turned red as a beet showing a mixture of excitement and adoration, as if Stu was her first love. Rhoda introduced Lynn and Stu at a party. Lynn could tell that Rhoda thought of Stu as a prize to be flaunted around to make all the women, especially Lynn jealous. To Rhoda's dismay, her plan backfired. Stu found Lynn irresistible and they had started to date. Eventually, they became an item around town.

Aunt Lynn had said the feeling of rejection that Rhoda experienced turned into hatred. Hatred not for Stu. How could anyone hate Stu? No, she had turned her contempt for her neighbor, Lynn. She was supposed to be her friend. Some friend.

Rhoda never forgot how Lynn "took her Stu away".

Nikki was brought back to the present and realized that Rhoda was droning on and on. She abruptly stopped when Heather came in holding a tray with coffee and the delectables.

"Well," Rhoda started again between bites of her eclair, "I suppose you are going sell the house now."

"What makes you think that?" Nikki snapped.

Heather looked at Nikki, puzzled as to why she had taken such a defensive tone.

In a softer tone, Nikki said, "As a matter of fact, we are planning to move in." Why?"

"Oh, just curious."

Yeah, so you can spread it all over town, I bet. Aloud, Nikki said, "We just sent for our things today."

"What about all of that horrible confusion. Thinking you killed your aunt!"

Oh no. Here we go again!

Before Nikki could respond, Heather wisely interrupted, "Oh, that. That was just some nonsense; a mistake, if you will. It's all cleared up now."

"So, now that Aunt Lynn is dead, will you be going out with Professor Waters?" Nikki felt a sense of triumph as she watch Rhoda blush with anger.

"Now look…"

"Nikki!" Heather turned to Rhoda. "I'm sure that Nikki didn't mean that the way it sounded. It's just that things have been so rough the last couple of days. And now, we're having to go through the house and determine what will be kept and what goes to the thrift store."

"By the way, Lynn had some pearls that I would like to have. Oh, and a diamond brooch." Rhoda didn't take her eyes off of Nikki as she sipped her coffee and waited for a response.

Both Nikki and Heather couldn't believe their ears. Lynn's body isn't even cold, and she over here asking for some of her things.

"My mother gave Aunt Lynn that brooch and the pearls were handed down to Aunt Lynn by her mother, who was given them by *her* mother."

"Yes. I believe those are the ones."

Rhoda had nerve. Could that be her only reason for this awkward visit? To get information and Aunt Lynn's jewels?

Heather looked at her watch. "Oh, gosh! Is that the time already? Don't you need to make some phone calls, Nikki?"

Nikki gave Heather a look of confusion.

Heather quickly said, "It's really good to meet you, Rhoda. Hope to see you soon."

Rhoda looked bewildered and more than a little disappointed. "Uh, yes. It's good to have you two living here. The manor would not be the same without a Johnson living here."

Rhoda extended her hand, gave them both a very limp handshake before walking down the path to the street.

"What dinner?"

Heather laughed, "That's the first thing that I thought of to get rid of her."

****

That evening, in the front living room, Heather and Nikki sat in front of the roaring fire with coffee.

Harry walked in, stretched his long frame and went to lie down next to Nikki. As the two friends were talking, his bigs ears moved back and forth. Though he seemed not to be paying any attention, Harry was listening intently.

"I wish I could think of where I put that receipt for Rick's Place. That could go a long way toward clearing you."

A hush fell over the room as the women were left with their own thoughts. They didn't notice Harry spring from the couch to the floor and prance over to Heather's purse. He stuck his head into it as far as he could, fished around and finally came up with the receipt from the coffee shop in his mouth.

He casually sauntered over to where Heather was now sprawled on the floor and dropped the slip of paper in front of her.

"What's this, Harry?" Heather picked up the receipt. Her beautiful aqua eyes flew wide open. She sat up quickly.

"Oh, my gosh. Look at this, Nikki. It's like he knew what we were talking about, but how could he know that it was in my purse? I looked for it in there myself and couldn't find it."

Nikki looked at Harry, who was nonchalantly grooming himself in front of the fireplace.

"I told you that he was amazing."

Heather scanned the receipt. "If the time is on this, it will prove that we weren't here at the time of death. Aha!" Heather turned the slip of paper toward Nikki. "See! Here it is. Now all we have to do is to turn this over to the sheriff and he'll have to believe us."

Nikki looked skeptical. "It proves that you were there, because you signed the receipt, but…"

"Look. There are two meals ordered and we were traveling together. Only a fool wouldn't make the connection."

Nikki closed her eyes to keep from crying in frustration. "Oh, what's the use. O'Neil will do anything to hang me for Aunt Lynn's murder."

As Nikki sat gazing at the fire, another thought came to mind.

She asked Heather, "What do you think about the idea of the Pink Diamond having something to do with Aunt Lynn's death?"

Heather looked at her friend dubiously. "You still don't even know if the legend is real, let alone how many, if any, people know about it or even believe it."

"I have heard a lot of different people around town talk about it. They have blown it all out of proportion until it became such a big mystery that some people actually speculated about where my uncle might have hidden it. Kids have been caught sneaking into the yard with spades and shovels to dig in the garden. When I was a kid, Tom and his brother Brian would come over to have 'treasure hunts' to see if we could find it." She paused while thinking about the theory. "It's just a thought. I know that Aunt Lynn trusted everyone in town and would think nothing of sharing the story of the Pink Diamond."

Harry jumped on the couch and crept across Nikki's lap three times and then stopped right in the middle, looked up at her with soulful eyes and meowed loudly.

Smiling, Nikki said, "Harry wants to go to bed." At that, the cat went barreling up the stairs and waited at the closed door for Nikki. She drained her last bit of coffee and pushed herself off of the couch. "I'm going up to read for a while. Goodnight."

Chapter 11

Saturday, December 15th

The next morning, Heather found Nikki hunched over the newspaper.

"It's on the front page."

"What is?" Heather poured herself some coffee.

"I am."

"What?" Heather moved closer and looked over Nikki's shoulder. She immediately saw the headlines in big, bold letters:

Heiress to Set Up Household in Harrot Manor

According to reliable sources, Nikki Johnson, who is the niece of and a suspect in the killing of Lynn Johnson, will be moving into Harrot Reef Manor.

"It goes on to say that I've just been released from jail pending further investigation." Nikki threw the paper down in disgust. "This is just short of libel!"

"I wonder who the 'source' is?"

They both knew...Rhoda.

"How long, I wonder, did it take her to report the story to the newspaper?"

"Not very long at all, since we only told her last night. She must have some friend on the paper," Nikki answered with disgust. Shaking her head, "Based on all Aunt Lynn told me about Rhoda, I should have known better than to tell that woman anything. She is known for twisting every story she hears until it is so far from the truth that it barely resembles the actual event."

Their discussion was interrupted by the doorbell.

"I'll get it." Nikki put her mug down and walked out of the room.

Tom was bending down to pick some paper off the porch. He handed it to Nikki.

"I believe this is for you."

Nikki took the envelope from Tom and opened the door wider and motioned for him to come in.

Entering the kitchen, Nikki said, "Look, Heather."

"What's that? Oh, hi, Tom."

Nikki turned the envelope over in her hand. "Hmm. There's no return address. It was just lying on the doorstep."

Nikki ripped the envelope, retrieved the note inside and hurriedly unfolded it. She immediately saw that the letters were cut out from books and magazines.

'Give it to me'.

Nikki passed it to Heather, confused.

Heather read it and looked up at Nikki, just as perplexed.

Tom read it. "Give what to who?"

Nikki shrugged her shoulders. "I have no idea."

"Nikki, what's going on" Tom asked.

Nikki looked defeated as she shrugged her shoulders in response.

"I think that you should call Greg," Tom said when Nikki was finally through. "Maybe he can run tests or something."

Heather reached in her back pocket for her cell and dialed Greg's direct line.

His deep, sexy voice came across the line. "Deputy Holloway."

"Greg…this is Heather. Nikki just received a strange letter." She waited, listening to what Greg was saying. "No postmark, no return address…in fact Nikki's address wasn't on it, just her name. Her given name, Nikki." She listened. "We have already handled it, so our fingerprints will be on it." Heather fell quiet again. "Yes, I know it was a stupid thing to do, but it all happened so fast. We really didn't think, I mean no one was suspecting something like this." Heather nodded her head and then ended the conversation with, "Okay. We will see you soon. Oh, and Greg…thanks. Bye."

"What did he say?"

"He will be over in a couple of minutes to look at it. I'm going to throw a pot of coffee on."

"I just came to say hi, but with all that's going on... I'll just leave it to Greg to take care of it, I'll see you later."

"I'm sorry, Tom," Nikki said.

Tom shook his head. No need to be. Just take care of yourself." Tom kissed Nikki's forehead and left.

Heather cleared her throat. "You might want to get dressed."

Nikki looked down and she saw that she still had her flannel nightgown on from the night before. She raced up the stairs, unpinning her tangled hair as she went.

Heather smiled and then the smile faded when she thought of what had just happened. They must have made someone nervous, but who? Before she had time to think more about it, the doorbell rang. She dried her hands and went to the door. Reaching her hand out, she stopped and decided to look to see who it was. Never can be too careful. Looking through the stain glass door didn't tell her anything, so Heather pulled the curtain that draped over the clear glass side panel next to the door. It was Greg, looking yummy as ever.

Heather opened the door. "Hi. I'm so glad that you were in when we called. I would have hated to talked to O'Neil. He wouldn't do anything anyway."

"You're probably right there." Greg seemed to be looking everywhere but at Heather, who was standing right in front of him.

"Coffee?"

"Hmm? Oh, please." He followed her into the kitchen. "So, where is Nikki? And the note?"

"Nikki's upstairs getting dressed and the note is right here. She's pretty upset about it."

Greg snatched it up from the breakfast table. He held it by the right corner only. "Habit," he said, sheepishly as Heather looked pointedly at him.

Greg stared at the note for a while.

"That's odd," Greg mumbled.

"What's that?" Nikki said, walking in the room.

Heather noticed the look on Greg's face when he saw Nikki come into the kitchen. Heather smiled to herself. Even though Nikki has had little or no sleep, she exuded the kind of beauty that men appreciated. Greg couldn't hide his admiration. Even with all of this going on, she still had a sort of sparkle about her.

Nikki's long legs were covered by designer jeans that fit like a glove. She wore a thin, white turtleneck under a baby blue mohair cardigan. Her long, damp, blond hair hung loose. She looked absolutely stunning, even with no make-up.

"Good morning, beautiful!"

It had slipped out before he could stop it. Nikki blushed.

Both women were looking at Greg with knowing smiles on their faces. Now it was his turn to blush.

He cleared his throat. "Yes…well. Back to business. You see here where this letter is shining and new. It's obviously from a new magazine, whereas this one," he pointed to the capital letter "G", "this is from a very old magazine. And these two are from two different books."

The women looked over his shoulders while he was explaining.

"So, what does that mean?" This came an anxious Nikki.

"I don't know." He watched her face fall. "Yet. I don't know yet. Let me take this back to the department. I'll send it to the lab and have some tests done. By then, we should have more of a handle on it."

Greg looked in her eyes and saw the fear that was reflected in them. He clasped her hands gently. With a soft voice, "I promise."

With that he tipped his hat to both of them and left.

After Greg left, Heather tried to get Nikki's mind off of the recent negative events.

"Should we start packing up Lynn's things today, so that we can make room for our belongings?"

Nikki refocused on the present and nodded.

Lately, Nikki found it so easy to hide in her memories of the past that it was difficult to stay in the present or, worse yet, look into the future.

"First, we need some boxes. Let's go to Abel's Grocery. They always have them in the back."

****

Their first stop was the grocery store. After rummaging for more cardboard boxes in the back, they went inside to buy the essentials needed for the pantry. It was Janet's day off, which made the tension that Nikki felt before stepping inside, drain from her body.

The tall, young man who checked them out, was painfully thin and no older than eighteen. His bright red hair was cut short and combed back away from his pimply face. His blue eyes were dull and watery.

He began handling the groceries, all the while sneezing, coughing and sniffling.

"Sounds like a terrible cold," Heather looked at his name tag, "Bruce. Shouldn't you be at home in bed?"

Bruce's only response was to sneeze. He bagged the rest of the food, took the money that Heather handed to him, and shoved the bags down at the end of the counter so that he could take care of the next customer. Nikki carefully placed the grocery bags in the basket and glared at him.

"Oh, no. Don't worry, I've got it," Heather said, all concern fell from her voice.

Sarcasm was lost on this kid.

The next stop was the *Ink and Quill* to get some packing supplies. The cashier was elderly, with gray hair swept up into a loose bun. Her green eyes were shining with joy and there were wrinkles around them from years of laughing. Beatrice was written in white block letters on the black name tag.

At least one person in town was full of Christmas spirit. Heather smiled at the beaming woman.

"Is someone moving at this time of year?" Beatrice asked while she bagged up the items that Nikki was buying.

Nikki smiled. "Well, yes...we are moving into the Harrot Reef Manor."

"Oh, then you must be Nikki. I'm sorry about your aunt, dear. Everybody in town adored her. She was so giving."

Nikki averted her eyes. She whispered, "Yes, she was. She loved this town, too."

"So, you are moving here? How nice that the manor will stay in the family."

"Yes, I would never sell it. I spent most of my childhood there. Anyway, it's what Aunt Lynn wanted."

Nikki paid for her things, picked up the bag and wished Beatrice a good day.

"Where to now?" Heather asked as she buckled her seatbelt.

Nikki checked her watch. They had picked up the supplies they needed for packing Aunt Lynn's things.

"One of the things that is bugging me is the tea. Where had it been purchased? Let's start looking around here."

"You know this town better than I," Heather answered.

"No, that's the problem. I really don't know the town anymore. There are so many new businesses."

Across the street, Nikki saw a good place to begin looking for the strange tea. Nikki indicated it with a slight nod of her head. "Over there is as good a place as any."

They walked across the street to "Viridity Herbs". Inside, they were met with a combination of overpowering smells. It took Nikki almost a minute before she could breathe freely. She rang the bell on the front counter and waited thirty seconds. No response. She rang it again. A woman of about of fifty came out from the back room.

"I'm sorry about the wait. I was on the telephone with a supplier."

Nikki and Heather both nodded politely. "It's okay. We understand." Nikki's answer was automatic.

"What can I get you today?"

Pulling the empty Pu-erh tea container from her purse, Nikki set it on the counter. "Do you happen to carry this kind of tea?"

The woman examined the box. "No, I don't, but I have heard of it. It's not very common here and it's very hard to find in the States. I'm sure you could order it online. You can get almost anything through the internet these days, can't you?"

"Do you have any idea where we can find it…besides the internet, that is? Is there a store around this area that might carry it?"

"Not that I know of. I think that you'd have to go to a big city. You know, like San Francisco or New York's Chinatown might have it."

Nikki blanched. That's just what O'Neil needed to hear to put another nail in her coffin. He knew that she lived in New York City.

"But you can't get it around here?" Heather asked.

"Well…you might try "The Dreamer" in Miller Cove. They may have it. If not, they may be able to tell you where you might get it. They may even be able to order it for you."

"Okay. Thank you."

The bell tinkled as they walked out the door. One down and who knows how many to go.

"Do you know where this "Dreamer" shop is?"

"Miller Cove," Nikki answered.

"I know that, but where exactly in Miller Cove?"

"I have no idea. It must be a new shop." Nikki started the motor and drove slowly down Main Street, in hopes that they would see another shop that might have it.

Heather pointed out her window. "What about that one?"

The store that she was indicating was tucked in a court off of Main Street.

Nikki shrugged. "Might as well take a look. It's a new one, so it will be interesting to know what they carry".

They parked the car in front of "Stargazer Health Food Store". They stopped just outside the door.

"No telling what they will have with a name like "Stargazer". Nikki said and smiled and pushed open the door.

A bell announced their arrival. There was a man behind the counter, reading a paperback. Looking around, Nikki could see that the place was empty.

Heather whispered, "I wonder how they stay in business. There are no customers." Nikki turned to her friend and smiled that crooked smile that drove men wild.

"Ladies, may I help you?"

Nikki stepped up to the counter and set the tea container down. "You wouldn't happen to carry this tea, would you, or know who does?"

"I used to carry it, but it didn't sell too well, so I didn't reorder it."

"How long ago was this?" Nikki was anxious now. Maybe they would get a clue as to who the killer was.

The man looked up to the ceiling and rubbed his bearded face. "Well, let me see. It was at least four months ago that I sold the last of it."

Nikki suddenly felt a pang of disappointment. If Aunt Lynn bought it herself then it must not have been the tea that killed her.

"Do you know Lynn Johnson?"

"Of course! Doesn't everyone know Lynn around here?"

"She was my aunt."

"Oh, that makes you Nikki. Lynn talked about you all of the time. I was really sorry to hear about what happened to her."

"Thank you." Nikki was getting impatient. "I was wondering if she used to buy that particular kind of tea here?"

"Oh, she bought all kinds of tea here."

"Yes, but she did buy *Pu-erh Tea* here?"

"Yes, but only once, maybe twice. As I said, I did not carry it too long. "

Nikki shoulders slumped. She had been beaten.

"How about somebody else?" Heather chimed in.

"Pardon?"

"I mean, was there anyone else who bought it?" Heather was getting just as frustrated as Nikki.

"A couple of tourists."

"Beside them."

"There might have been a local or two, but I don't remember."

"Can we look at your receipts?" Heather was hoping that Nikki had some pull in this town. Her family founded Harrot Reef, after all.

"Well, no. I'm sorry, but I can't show those to you. Privacy, and all that, you know."

Crestfallen, there was nothing else they could do here. Unless someone had bought it somewhere out of town, Aunt Lynn must have bought it herself.

"Is there something else that I can help you with. Would you like some nice ginger tea? Or maybe chocolate mint? It is a favorite this time of the year."

Heather shook her head. The two friends turned to leave.

Heather called over her shoulder, "No, thank you. We are a couple of coffee girls. Thanks anyway."

They waited until they got into the car to talk. Nikki started the motor and within minutes the heater was blowing hot air on them.

"Now what? Do we go to that town that the woman in the first shop told us about?"

Nikki was quiet. "It's no use," she said at last. "Aunt Lynn probably bought the tea herself, and it was just coincidence that it was left on the counter the other night."

Heather kept quiet about the possibility that someone poisoned it. No sense upsetting her more.

Nikki slammed the car into gear, causing it to jerk Heather out of her reverie. "Oh, come on. Let's go get something to eat. I've had enough of this for one day. Aunt Lynn had a heart attack, and that was it."

Heather looked at her in disbelief. "Nikki. You don't really believe that do you?" She got no response.

There it was again. That nagging feeling that Nikki had something to do with all of this. Could she have really killed Lynn for the money and then used Heather as a convenient witness? Heather shook her head. No. That was not the Nikki that she knew. But…did we ever *really* know anyone?

Chapter 12

Sunday, December 16th

"Heather, you want to take a break?"

They were working on getting the house together, after all they were going to have a memorial service in a week and the house needed to be thoroughly cleaned from top to bottom. They braced themselves against the freezing wind and hurried to the diner door. At the counter they spied Rhoda who was talking a mile a minute.

Nikki heard her say, "…and now that she's dead, don't you think he'll come back to me?"

The question went unanswered as Martha turned her attention to Nikki and Heather as they walked in out of the cold.

Hearing the bell ring over the door ring, Rhoda turned and saw her neighbors. She slowly began to turn red, as if she were caught saying something that she knew she shouldn't. The problem with Rhoda was that, even though she knew that she shouldn't, she couldn't keep herself from gossiping. She was the town gossip and saw it as her duty to keep everyone informed about the latest news because she was the head of the rumor mill.

"Hi, girls," Martha grabbed the coffee pot and came around the counter. "As you can see, it's in between the rush hours. Take your pick of tables."

As soon as they sat down, Rhoda swooped in, bringing tension with her. "So, how are you, Nikki?" Her voice was dripping with insincere concern.

"Okay, Rhoda. We are…"

She jumped in. "It is all so terrible. I mean, your aunt dying like that and then for you to be blamed? I still can't believe it! Well, I don't know if I could take it if I were you! I mean…"

"Rhoda. She's fine," Heather said. "In fact, we are settling in nicely."

"Oh…" The hesitation expressed the disappointment that Rhoda felt… "Well, that's nice." Trying to hide her true feelings, she followed with, "You have to come for tea one day soon."

Nikki couldn't help but to roll her eyes. *When pigs fly!*

When her suggestion fell on deaf ears, Rhoda finally got the hint and excused herself, walking away in a huff.

When Rhoda was gone, Heather shook her head. "Can you believe the nerve? She's just looking for more scandal to spread."

Martha came to refill their cups.

"Martha, who was Rhoda talking about when we came in?"

"Oh, I don't know. Does it matter?" For a few moments, Nikki saw the otherwise calm Martha get flustered.

"Come on. Was it Aunt Lynn?"

"Yes," was her muttered response.

"So, what kind of garbage was she spreading?"

"Nikki. You really don't want to know."

"Yes. I do. Now spill it."

"She was just talking about Stu and your aunt," Martha said.

"Yesss…and?"

"Just about how she hated her for what she did."

"You mean, how Aunt Lynn supposedly stole him away from her?" Nikki asked incredulously.

"Yeah."

"Hate is a pretty strong word. What else, Martha? I heard her saying something about Aunt Lynn dying." Nikki wouldn't let it go.

"Oh, you know Rhoda. Sometimes she says things without thinking. Forget it, Nikki. It really isn't important."

"Martha. What was it that she said about when Aunt Lynn died?"

"Nothing. I mean, that's when you came in and she stopped talking. Now, can I get you girls something to eat?"

They both shook their heads and Martha hurried away.

"Well, that's all we're going to get for now," Nikki said with disappointment.

****

That evening, Harry was sulking about. He needed for Nikki and Heather to work together, but, it was obvious to Harry that Heather was beginning to distrust Nikki. He knew she didn't want to, but things just kept on piling up against Nikki. It was magnified when she told Heather that she occasionally brought the tea up here as a surprise for Lynn.

Harry knew that Heather didn't want to believe that Nikki could hurt a fly, but she needed proof. *Okay...she wanted proof, he'll give it to her*. He suddenly developed a determined look.

Harry jumped on the counter and stood on his hind legs. Once again, he was glad for his size. He reached up, grabbed the knob on the cupboard door and gave it a yank. Harry jumped on the first shelf, sending boxes of tea everywhere. He jumped down, found the one that he wanted, and played field hockey with it until Heather came in.

"Harry! What in the world are you up to?"

Harry skittered to another box and pounced on it, sending it flying across the room.

"Alright, Harry. That's enough!"

"Trill."

Heather knew from recent experience that "trill" meant that she had missed something— something that was most likely important. She picked up the two boxes that Harry seemed to be playing with, and read the contents.

"Well, what do you know?"

"Trill." Harry turned and walked away.

Nikki came down the stairs, taking two at a time. She got as far as the kitchen and stopped cold when she saw the mess on the floor.

"What the heck...?"

"Don't look at me. Harry did it."

"Sure, Heather. Blame the cat."

"No, really. I heard all this commotion coming from the kitchen. I came in and Harry was playing with the boxes. He especially liked these two."

Heather showed Nikki the two boxes in question. They were two different brand names of Pu-erh tea. One box was opened, and was the one that Heather saw on the first night.

Indicating the other box, Nikki exclaimed, "This box is the one I gave her the last time I was here. I can tell by the brand."

"It obviously wasn't the one that was poisoned."

"What are you saying? That I would try to kill Aunt Lynn?"

Heather started backpedaling. "No. I just meant that someone else couldn't have poisoned that tea."

"Oh, Heather. I'm sorry. I know that you could never think that I..."

"No. I couldn't."

Heather put her arms around her dear friend and silently chastised herself again for thinking that Nikki could kill her aunt.

Chapter 13

Monday, December 17th

Early the next morning, Nikki decided to see Aunt Lynn's doctor, Dr. C. Sweeney.

The empty reception room was warm with dark wooden paneling. Two comfortable couches sat in the corner with a round glass coffee table in front of them. The receptionist was behind a pane of frosted glass.

Nikki walked to the desk and rapped lightly on the glass. The receptionist slid open the glass pane. The look on her face told Nikki that this lady wanted to be anywhere but here.

"Hi, I'm Nikki Johnson. Doctor Sweeney was my aunt's doctor. May I speak with him regarding my Aunt Lynn's death, please?"

Nikki was ushered in immediately.

"Hi, Nikki. It's been a while. How are you holding up?"

"I'm okay. It's hard, but I know that Aunt Lynn wouldn't want me to mourn too long."

Dr. Sweeney indicated a chair across the desk and Nikki gratefully sat down. She hadn't realized, until now, just how tired she was after another fitful night of sleep.

"So, what can I do for you?"

"It's about my Aunt Lynn. Can you tell me about her health? I know it's against the law while a patient is alive, but since she is dead, and I'm her only living relative, I thought...", she left the comment unspoken.

After a long pause, Dr. Sweeney said, "Well, since Lynn is dead...I suppose it won't hurt. Marge," he spoke through the intercom, "please bring Lynn Johnson's file in."

Marge came in holding a thick file with her aunt's name on the tab and the word DECEASED scrawled on the front in red ink. Nikki's breath caught in her throat as she let out a little gasp. The doctor looked up from Lynn's file to see Nikki's troubled face. He quickly placed the file, face down, on his desk.

He studied the paper that he pulled from the file. He looked up over his reading glasses at an anxious Nikki.

"Your aunt suffered from high blood pressure, but not so high that it would be a likely cause of her death. She didn't want to take medication, so she tried alternative medications. She drank Pu-erh Tea."

"Yes, yes. I know all that. Doctor, does Pu-erh tea have a strong odor?"

"Why, yes it does, extremely strong, in fact." The doctor cleared his throat and continued, "Lynn was active...still running 5 miles a day up until the last month, she ate in a healthy manner, never smoked, and drank nothing but water and tea. If she drank enough of that Pu-erh tea, like say more than 4 cups a day, it might make her very sick but would be an unusual cause of death, although among other chemicals this tea has, it also contains small amounts of arsenic."

"Was there enough arsenic to kill her?"

"Like I said, if she drank enough it could make her very sick, but it would be doubtful this could contribute to death. Your aunt knew that she could only drink one cup a day. Lynn was very cautious about what she put in her body."

Nikki shook her head. "Then I don't understand. If she had nothing wrong with her medically, except for the high blood pressure, which you claim would be unlikely to have been the cause of her death, then what happened? What was the cause of her death?"

"I'm sorry. I don't know. We'll just have to wait until I receive the toxicology report, but if that comes back without an apparent answer, sometimes we never know for sure what a cause of death might be."

"So you'll get the report?"

"Yes I will. As soon as I get it, I'll let you know."

Nikki got up from the chair, reached across the desk, and shook the doctor's hands.

"I'll be looking forward to that. Thank you for your time and the information."

With that, she turned and left the office.

****

After coming home from Dr. Sweeney's office, Nikki thought that the best thing for her to do would be to start working again. She poured a fresh cup of coffee, got out her laptop, and sat down at the desk in the library. The library was filled with ghosts of the other night. She could still see her aunt lying on the floor. She knew that she couldn't write in this room. So, she picked up her coffee and her computer and made her way to the desk in the upstairs study. There she found peace and quiet.

Nikki opened her email and went through each correspondence. Most of them were from the magazines for which she was freelancing for pay while writing her mystery novel. She opened one that had the subject line: The Study of Cults and Their Influence on World Cultures. Thinking that it was some information for her novel that she was writing, she read it through and immediately let out a gasp.

If you don't give it to me, you'll be sorry!

Nikki called for Heather. "Look at this. I just found this in my email!"

Heather read the email quickly. "This is like the note from the other day. I wonder who it's from and what they are looking for. What could your aunt have had that someone would want?"

"I have no idea. I don't think my aunt had any secrets, and even if she did I would not know the first place to look."

"That note that we found on the porch and this email probably are connected in some way. All we have to do is figure out who sent them and what they want," Heather said.

"The problem is that I'm not sure how to find out what they want."

Heather took the situation in hand. "Well, there is only one thing to do."

Nikki looked at her expectantly.

Heather said matter-of-factly, "We need to let Greg see this."

"I'm not sure that he can do anything about this. It's not like he could check handwriting analysis, It's an email." Nikki sounded beat.

"I know; but he might be able to trace it back to the computer that the writer used," Heather said hopefully.

The doorbell sounded and the women looked up and then at each other. Nikki rose from her chair and went down the stairs hesitantly she opened the door. On the other side of the door was a bouquet of dead flowers.

"Oh, my gosh! Who are they from? Don't tell me, let me guess. The person who is looking for something that you don't have." Heather rushed toward the door.

"I don't know. They were left on the doorstep there's a card." Nikki took the small card out of the envelope. It read:

Guess Who?

Nikki dropped the flowers and they fell to the floor. She stared at the card.

"What does it say?"

Heather came to Nikki's side and read the card over her shoulder.

"Well, now we really need to get Greg over here."

The doorbell rang five minutes after Heather hung up with Greg.

Heather opened the door to Greg, and before he step over the threshold said, "Hi. How's Nikki?" He didn't wait to be asked in.

"She's pretty shaken up. I mean, getting the two threats within 15 minutes of one another. It was timed so perfectly. As if he was watching her and knew her routine."

"Routine?" Greg asked.

"Yeah, I mean Nikki always goes through her emails first, and then begins to work. She opened an emailed threat and about 5-10 minutes later, the doorbell rang. We found these laying on the porch with this card."

Greg took the card from Heather and read it.

"This is interesting. It doesn't refer to whatever is wanted, like the others have."

"What do you mean?" Heather looked over his shoulder and studied the card again.

"Well, like one said something about giving something to him. This is like he's trying to scare the heck out of you."

"He's doing a pretty good job." Nikki walked into the kitchen. "Hi, Greg. What do you think?"

"I don't know yet. I need to see the email."

Greg followed the girls upstairs to the upstairs study. He spied the desk and the laptop on top of it.

"Here." Nikki led the way to the roll top desk. "The subject line said 'Manuscript'. I thought it was information for the book that I'm working on."

Greg read the missive twice. When he had finished, he turned around to the women, with a concerned look in his eyes.

"Have you been telling anyone about what's happening?"

"We just talked to Tom about it the other day, but that was only because he was there when I received the last note."

Greg was filled with exasperation. "What part of 'don't talk about this to anyone else' don't you understand? How can I keep you safe if you won't follow orders?"

Nikki came to life. "What do you mean orders? You can't order me around. I need to find out who killed my aunt and why. The Sheriff's Office doesn't seem to want to do anything about this."

"Nikki we do... I do care. That's why I am helping."

"Helping? You call this helping?" Nikki was close to tears.

Heather sighed. "Nikki, why do you have to be..."

"Be *what?*" Nikki turned on Heather.

"Don't be so one way about it. We are all on the same side. Why can't we just continue to work together? You know that we cannot do it alone. O'Neill may not want to help you, but Greg does and we need to let him."

Nikki calmed down and finally gave in. "Okay."

Heather breathed a sigh of relief. Finally, Nikki is listening to reason again.

Chapter 14

Tuesday, December 18th

Nikki's cell rang just as she was getting out of the shower. She moaned. "Why can't I take a shower in peace?" she asked Harry.

"Trill."

Harry had followed her into the bathroom, and was sitting next to the tub, guarding Nikki from all evil.

Quickly dressing in a pair of jeans and a grey sweatshirt with a Maine Coon cat decal that looked curiously like Harry, Nikki gathered her wet hair into a bun. She walked to her bed, where the cell was ringing again.

"Hello?"

"Nikki? This is Tom."

"Hi, Tom. What's up?"

"I was wondering…er, well…do you have any plans for tonight?"

"No. Why?"

"I would like to take you to The White Sands for dinner?"

Nikki thought about it. Would she be leading Tom on if she accepted?

"I'll go on one condition."

"What's that?" Tom's voice was full of hope.

Nikki cringed. Was she doing the right thing?

"I'll go *if* you promise that it's just as friends, nothing more."

Nikki could hear the disappointment in Tom's voice, but he agreed, "Just friends."

****

Nikki said, as she settled in the passenger seat, "It was nice of Brian to let us use his truck tonight. He's a good brother."

"Well, he owed me. I'm the one who got this old heap running. Besides, he never uses it except to haul garbage." Tom smiled as he waited for the engine to turn over. The truck was a beat-up 1969 Chevy C10 that had seen better days, but Brian got it for a song. He wondered why it was so cheap until six months down the road the transmission blew. It took Tom and him both a month to get it back on the road.

"I suppose the garbage doesn't need to be warm," Nikki chuckled. She wrapped her powder blue parka tight around herself.

Tom laughed and turned on the heater. "Just wait a minute. It'll blast us out of here."

The night was frigid and the snow drifts were at least three feet high. The road was freshly salted to help the old truck's tires gain traction.

Tom changed gears, and Nikki could hear them grinding in rebellion. She instinctively grabbed hold of the dashboard to keep her from flying off her seat. The truck stalled when Tom stopped at the stop sign on Main Street and Gull Harbor Road.

"You did a great job of getting this old heap to run." Nikki laughed, gave him a friendly fist bump on his arm. At that moment her eyes danced in the street lamp, her laughter reaching her eyes. At that moment, Nikki felt the happiest she had since she had arrived here. It was almost like the past few days were a horrible nightmare.

He finally felt the engine grab and turn over.

"Yes!" Turning to Nikki, he said, "See. I told you I could get it running again."

In between laughter, she said, "No, you didn't say that at all. What you said was that you were the one who got this old heap running. All I want to know is when will you get this old heap to run without stalling out? Hmm?"

Suddenly, there was a horn blaring behind them. "Oops. I guess we better move it, now that this old heap is actually running." Tom smiled, looked at Nikki with a wink, and put it in gear, grinding them as he did.

"Tom! The restaurant is back there!"

"Oh, no!" Tom turned around in another lot. "I was just testing you."

"Oh, and did I pass?"

"With flying colors," said with another wink before parking the truck.

He abruptly left the warmth when he opened the door to face the frigid air of Winter. He moved quickly as he walked around to help Nikki get out. It was a beautiful night. There were a thousand stars in the sky and the moon was full. He gazed over at the gorgeous woman next to him.

"What?"

Tom was brought out of his reverie. "What 'what'?"

"What are you smiling at?"

"Am I smiling?"

"Yeah. Your teeth are showing."

"They are?" He felt his face and responded, "So they are."

They both broke into laughter as Tom held the door open for Nikki. He stepped up to the reception desk and lowered his voice. The maitre d' nodded, picked up two menus and escorted them to the finest table in the house. Nikki's eyes grew wide with excitement. After he helped her with her chair, the maitre d' turned to Tom and nodded. He then faded into the background.

Nikki looked around her with appreciation. There was a floor-to-ceiling window on the far left side of the restaurant. The view was breathtaking. She could see the last bit of smoky color of the sunset. The harbor lights were twinkling, making the recently fallen snow sparkle. There were a few tourists that were braving the knife-splitting cold to walk along the boardwalk.

Nikki turned her gaze on Tom and caught him looking at her with adoration in his eyes. Her eyes quickly avoided his. She, instead looked behind him to another floor-to-ceiling window with a different view of the harbor.

Nikki's eyes took this opportunity to take in the rest of the sights. Tom's was dressed in a fresh white shirt covered with a brown cable-knit sweater. His wavy chestnut hair was a wind blown mess, but somehow it suited him. His eyes were like pools of dark chocolate. His smile was enough to make her forget they were only friends.

The waiter walked up to the table with a chilled bottle of champagne. Nikki's hands flew to her mouth, covering the little sound of surprise. Tom looked at her and laughed.

As the waiter poured, Nikki wriggled nervously. "What is this all about, Tom? Champagne is for special occasions."

"Don't you know that any time spent with you is a special occasion?"

"Yeah, right." She rolled her eyes.

"No, really. Every time I am with you, it just seems like we are the only people on earth."

"Tom." Nikki gave him that look he knew so well. "Slow down. We are…"

"Only friends," Tom chimed in. "Yeah, I know, but I just keep thinking about the times we spent together when we were kids. We had a lot of laughs, didn't we?"

Nikki slowly nodded her head. "Yes, but we were just kids then."

"So?"

Nikki looked out at the harbor. She lowered her voice. "So, now we're not." She dared to gaze over to her friend and saw the crushed look in his beautiful eyes. She reached across the table and took his hand.

"Oh, Tom. You know it would never work. We've been friends for too long. Let's not destroy our friendship by taking a chance on a romantic relationship."

"So…what then? Do you think that Greg can make you happy?"

"Wait…Greg? Is that what you think?" Nikki snatched her hand back. "You are way off base. Greg is nothing but a means to an end, and he knows it, too. Besides, Greg isn't looking for a relationship. For your information, his wife just passed away less than a year ago."

"Oh, really? I've seen the way he looks at you. All moony-eyed."

"Oh, Tom. You are being ridiculous. Let's drop it and enjoy a lovely evening."

Tom reached for her hand this time, and gazed into her blue eyes.

"How I have missed you. How often have I wished that I never let you leave."

"Tom, I've missed you, too, but I'm a changed person."

"You seem like the same old Nikki to me. Beautiful, sensitive, funny..."

Nikki pulled her hand from his. "Stop!" She had a twinkle in her eye as she admonished him. "I just want to have a nice evening with an old friend. Nothing more."

She felt the sudden tension in the air, and felt guilty for taking, what could have been a great evening, and turning it into a disaster. From the look on Tom's face he felt the change in mood. He turned away from her gaze. The magic of the evening was lost, and poor Tom didn't know what happened to it. It seemed that her words had crushed him.

In a voice that was just above a whisper, she said, "Tom, I don't mean to hurt you. There is something that happened in New York... well it opened my eyes to a lot of things."

He whipped his head around to look at her, "What happened, Nikki?"

A silence that seemed to last forever came over them, and then Nikki got up the courage to talk about the most painful time of her life, up until her aunt passed.

"About six months ago, I was supposed to marry a stock broker named David. We were so in love and happy together...or so I thought." She stopped long enough to take a sip of champagne. "On our wedding day, I waited to walk down the aisle, but I never made it there."

"Why?"

She lowered her eyes so that he couldn't see them well up with tears. "He didn't show," she whispered.

"Did you ever find out why?"

With her eyes still lowered, "Yes." Nikki got her control back and regarded him for a moment before she answered, "He was already married."

Tom's mouth dropped, eyes wide. "Oh, Nikki. I'm so sorry. Was there any clue? I mean, how long were you together?"

"A year. At the time, I really didn't notice anything amiss, but afterward, when I looked back…" She gazed off in the distance, recalling something so painful that she could hardly talk about it. "When I looked back, a lot of things came to mind that should have raised a red flag."

"Like?"

"Like breaking dates…a lot of dates. Asking, no, telling me not to call his home number because "he was away from home too much." So, like the idiot I am, trusted him and never questioned him. Not once."

"It's not your fault that he was…is...a jerk. Although, you *are* too trusting. You always were, even in school. That's one of the things that I love about you, but I was always afraid that you would get burned."

"That's an understatement if ever I heard one. It's bad enough getting stood up for the Senior Ball…"

"Did you get stood up? Who were you going to go with?"

"Hugh French."

"Oh, he was a jerk, too."

"Now you tell me," she said, laughing.

The mood was lightened again and Tom refilled their glasses. They laughed and talked about old times as they ate their lobsters.

Later, on her doorstep, Tom gently put his hand on her arm. She turned to him, her pale blue eyes shone in the moonlight. They stood there, in the still night, and Tom bent down and kissed her forehead.

"Goodnight." With that, he turned and started down the icy path.

"Thank you," she called after him. He didn't reply.

Chapter 15

Wednesday, December 19th

The following day, after receiving the boxes of their personal effects, Heather and Nikki decided that they would go upstairs to the attic. That was the only room in the house left to go through. They went up the stairs and found the door locked.

"Oh, yeah. Aunt Lynn use to always keep this door locked. Don't ask me why. When we were kids, we thought that there was a monster hiding inside." Shaking her head at the memory, Nikki let out a little laugh. "You stay here and I'll go get the key."

Harry wound his body around Heather's legs, purring. Within minutes, Nikki returned with the key. She tried to ease it into the lock, but it stopped halfway through. The lock was stuck.

"Maybe it's rusted," Heather suggested. "We might have to get a locksmith out here."

Heather was trying to help, she knew, but Nikki was exasperated just the same. The last thing that she wanted to do was to wait for a locksmith. Nikki jiggled the old skeleton key impatiently once again and, just when she was about to give up, it suddenly gave way. The door creaked as it slowly opened. Harry scooted by them and into the room, where he plopped his considerable body down in front of the bookcase against the wall.

The attic was unlike any other. It was divided into two parts by a peak in the roof line. Instead of boxes, and old furniture, as in most other attics, this one had a quaint little studio apartment, set up with a bathroom and separate sitting and sleeping areas on one side and a small office with an old roll top desk on the other.

"Did you know that this was here?" Heather asked.

Nikki realized that her mouth was open in surprise. As she stood in one place, turning, she answered, "No, I had no idea. Remember I told you that we thought it was where a monster lived. I guess as I got older, I didn't give it much thought."

Nikki moved to the side of the attic that served as a sitting area and stood in a puddle of sunlight. Even though there was no fire up here, she could still feel the warmth of the sunshine. She could see that it had been quite a while since anyone had been up here as the dust was floating in the air.

Nikki sat on the couch, picked up a magazine and leafed through it. She felt as though she went back in time 40 years. In the magazine there were articles about the Vietnam war ending and the Lebanese war starting.

Across the room were a stack of old vinyl records. She picked up the top record and saw that it was by the band America and it was their first album. Nikki turned it over and found that it was out in 1975. Next to the stack of records was an old record player, circa 1960.

"This is weird. A magazine *and* a record, both dated 1975. I wonder what else we can find around here?"

They started to go through the whole attic, inch by inch. There was nothing else in the sitting area, but the office turned up a few things. Heather opened the desk to find cubby holes full of old bills, receipts and a letter.

On the front of the sealed envelope, was simply penned, "Nikki" in her aunt's handwriting. She opened it and started to read about a side of her family that she didn't know. How one of her relatives went crazy and lived in the attic for a year before commiting suicide by shooting himself up there. They never could get the blood stain out of the floor, so they covered it with a rug. After that, no one was allowed up there. At the very end of the letter, she said something which Nikki thought peculiar. Her aunt told Nikki to be careful and watch Harry. He knows more than you think.

Harry stopped grooming himself suddenly and regarded them both with knowing eyes. It looked as though he was smiling. He certainly had a secret, but would he reveal it?

****

Later that day, Nikki suggested that they take a break from getting the house in order.

They turned into the parking of lot of Martha's just as the snow started whipping around in the wind. Nikki and Heather rushed in to Martha's. Stomping the snow off their feet and blowing through their cupped, gloved hands, they waited to catch Miranda's eye. The little diner was busy with the lunch crowd and the cacophony of voices rose with laughter from every corner in the room. Martha's daughter, Miranda, hurried toward them, menus in hand.

The fresh-faced girl was obviously flustered, and who wouldn't be with all of these customers. Looking around, Nikki saw that there wasn't another wait person on the floor.

Miranda's straight blond hair was tied up off of her neck, leaving a few strands that escaped, to cascade down her neck to her shoulders. She was flushed with the heat that comes from running from table to table, filling up coffee cups and delivering orders.

"Sorry it took so long. The new guy had an emergency and had to leave. If you ask me, it wasn't his wife that needed him, but he just wanted to get away from all of these people," Miranda complained.

"So, he's not working out either, eh?" Nikki clucked softly. "Why is it that your mom can't get good help? Jobs are hard to come by, you'd think that once they get the job, they would do anything to keep it."

Miranda just shrugged her thin shoulders, swept a strand of hair from her face, and turned around. "Come on this way. There's a table that just opened up," she threw over her shoulder.

Once they sat down, Miranda handed them their menus. "The special today is the Fisherman's Stew. Rod brought in a bunch of beautiful salmon this morning."

"Sounds great. I'll have that and a cup of coffee, too, please." Heather handed Miranda the menu.

"Nikki?"

"Make that two. I've missed your mom's stew."

"Okay, got it. I'll get your coffee right now."

Nikki shrugged off her coat. "I finally got warm. It seems like it's colder today."

Heather quietly nodded. "It's all that wind, and then the snow on top of that."

"Hi, ladies."

Nikki looked up to see Greg and Robert standing next to their table.

"May we join you?"

Heather nodded. "Of course."

After Miranda took the guys' order, Greg leaned in and lowered his voice. "So, I confirmed that Stu Waters had fought with your aunt the night before she died."

"What about?" Nikki asked.

"According to Rhoda, whose version is somewhat suspect, there was another woman. I also talked to Martha, who knows everything in this town, and she said she thought there was another woman on the side, but she didn't know who."

"So, how do we find out?" Nikki whispered.

"We need to keep our eyes and ears open. Someone's got to know something and they'll slip up sometime."

Miranda had silently filled coffee cups around the table. While she appeared nonchalant, she was taking in every word. She would have to let Stu know that he was under investigation and that soon their secret could be blown wide open.

****

It seemed to Miranda that the rest of the day was in slow motion. She needed to get to the college as soon as possible to get to Stu before Greg could. Stu needed to be warned so they could keep their stories straight to prevent their secret from slipping out.

Dewey sat next to the door of Martha's, waiting for something good to happen. He sat there for what seemed like hours, until he saw Miranda hurriedly donning her scarf, coat and gloves.

Oh, boy! Now comes the action. Dewey sprinted across the parking lot, lept into the bed of Miranda's pickup truck and crawled under a tarp, out of sight.

Miranda parked the car in the college parking lot. Dewey waited until Miranda was well ahead of him, then began to follow her.

Miranda turned up her collar against the bitter cold. Reaching for the handle on the cafeteria door, she played tug of war with the wind, and finally opened it, throwing herself off balance. Once she was inside, she let the door bang shut behind her. She liked this cafeteria. It had a sort of split personality. It was actually two rooms in one, with a half wall in the middle.

The left side contained everything that you would expect to see in a cafeteria, including a buffet, salad bar, and drink dispensers, all help-yourself. The tables were wooden and scarred from years of use. Chairs were scattered everywhere in the room, each at no table particular. The students were celebrating the end of the term. Their raised voices filled the air, bouncing off the walls.

As Miranda approached the other room, she was conscious of her heels tapping on the damp tile floor. She stopped at the doorway, and scanned the room, hoping to see Stu.

Of course, Miranda thought, he was never where he was supposed to be. While she was waiting for the student to take her to her table, she took in the ambiance of the room. The two sides of the cafeteria were like night and day. The first difference that Miranda noticed was the lighting. While the casual side had harsh, glaring light, to make it easier for students to study, the "restaurant side" was darker, easier on the eyes. The tables on this side were covered with white linen tablecloths and each table had pretty crystal bud vases in the center. Today's flower was a single red rose. Instead of plastic "silverware", there were place settings of stainless on black cloth napkins. The design of the room was modern monochromatic, with black and white sketches in silver frames. The carpeting was dark in color, and softened the footsteps of the young woman that approached Miranda.

"Hi. Is it just you today?" The young girl had a knowing twinkle in her eye.

Miranda tried to keep from blushing. "No. I'm meeting someone. I guess he'll be here a little later."

The waitress nodded respectfully at Miranda, trying to slip back into her professional mode. She led the way to a table in a dark corner.

Dewey had sneaked in through the fast-paced, noisy kitchen, so no one noticed the cat as he did his greatest snake impression, and slithered behind the plant close to where Miranda sat. He had a bird's eye view of the table from where he was stationed, and his keen sense of hearing made it easy to hear the conversation.

"Hello."

Miranda looked up to find Stu standing beside her. Her heart skipped a beat, just like it did the first day that she saw him.

She flashed back to the first day of the term and he was lecturing on Hemingway, who happened to be one of Miranda's favorite authors. Stu paced back and forth in the front, instead of using the podium. He seemed to think better when he moved about.

Miranda found her thoughts drifting. The professor's voice droned on, but she had stopped listening. Instead she was thinking of his hazel eyes, which captivated her. His silver-colored hair made him look distinguished, even mysterious. Suddenly, his tall, lanky body was standing over her. She could smell the slightly woodsy scent of his aftershave.

Stu had asked her something. What was it? She looked into his smoldering eyes, aware that the whole class was waiting for her to answer his question.

"I'm sorry. What was the question?"

He rolled his eyes and looked beyond her at another student, who answered without hesitation.

Miranda was crestfallen. She had one chance to dazzle him with her knowledge about Hemingway, and she blew it. The period ended, and she stood, gathering her books. Professor Waters approached her and began speaking in his low, gravelly voice.

""Miss Kaiser?"

Miranda felt her face turn beet red. "Yes?"

"What happened back there? Was my lecture that boring?"

Miranda was quick to reply. "No. Not at all. I'm so sorry. It won't happen again."

****

That was six months ago. Since then, they had enjoyed a companionship like no other. Miranda had reached the point where she wanted more. The more she wanted, the further away Stu got. She wanted him to love her, to need her as much as she needed him, but Lynn had come along and, for reasons that she couldn't fathom, he was distracted by her. He was hooked, and Miranda had to settle with being "the other woman".

"Hi. How was class?" Miranda tried to act as normal as possible, even though she felt as though she was going to jump out of her skin. She tried, unsuccessfully, to stop squirming.

"Fine. What's up? Why did you want to meet?"

Miranda tried to hide the pain she felt inside. She often found herself asking why he wanted to be with her. Was it because of the danger? Maybe the possibility of getting caught by Lynn that excited him. Now that Lynn was dead, their relationship had turned from a roaring fire to smoldering embers. Now, she felt herself walking on eggshells whenever she was around him.

"Besides finding out how you are, I wanted to warn you."

"Warn me? About what?" Stu said irritably.

Dewey's ears twitched.

"I just came from work. Nikki and Heather were in and I overheard them talking about suspects in Lynn's murder."

"Yeah, so?"

She knew that Stu was naturally impatient, and in the mood he was in, she only had a few minutes before he would explode.

"They think that you might have done it. In fact, you are their prime suspect."

"What?" Stu was about to lose it. This was all he needed.

Miranda quickly pointed out that she was his alibi, which meant that he would be hers. "This way, we are both off the hook."

"Yeah, but I don't necessarily want the whole town knowing about us."

Miranda looked at him painfully. Was he that embarrassed by her? Was it because she was so much younger than he?

Stu caught her expression. He reached across the table and took her hand to give it a quick squeeze and then, just as fast, he pulled his hand away, looking around to make sure that no one saw the gesture.

"Don't you see? If O'Neil or Holloway found out about us, instead of helping me, it would put me in the spotlight as the only suspect. Considering my relationship with Lynn, they might think that you are my reason for getting her out of the way."

Slowly, Miranda came to understand what exactly he meant. "So what do we do? Lie?"

"Let me think about it."

"Stu, we have an alibi that can be verified by the waitress at the White Sands. We can just say that we were out discussing my dissertation."

"How many professors take their students out to the most expensive place in town to discuss the student's dissertation?"

Dewey sighed. One suspect accounted for.

****

The four friends had just left Martha's.

"Are you sure you won't go out with me? Come on, Heather. Just one little date."

Robert danced around her as they walked down the street. Up ahead, Nikki and Greg were strolling with their heads together as they talked intently.

Heather giggled. "Robert, stop acting like you're in high school. I don't feel right leaving Nikki alone right now."

"Aw, she's a big girl. Besides she has Greg to keep her company."

Heather silently shook her head. Robert opened his mouth to protest once again, and she stopped, raised her hand for him to stop taking.

"Please, Robert. No more."

As she moved passed him, he laid his hand on her arm. She couldn't help herself. She found her eyes locking on his.

He whispered, "Coffee? Please?"

"Oh, ok. But just coffee, nothing more."

Pleased that she finally gave in to him, he grinned like a kid. He tried to slip his arm around her waist. She wriggled out of his grasp.

"Just coffee."

They agreed to meet at Martha's the following day at 10:00, after the breakfast rush.

Chapter 16

Thursday, December 20th

The next morning, Heather opened her eyes, stretched and then remembered the promise that she had made to Robert the night before.

"Oh no," she groaned. To Harry, she asked, "What was I thinking?" Harry looked at Heather and meowed his response.

A voice inside her head kept asking, "What do you really know about him?"

She dragged herself out of bed, resigned to make the most of it. Robert really wasn't *that* bad. Oh, sure. He was a little full of himself, but he was charming and fun to be with. It's not like a real date, like dinner at the White Sands, which would be convenient for him, as it is in a hotel. That would be the limit. She decided to make the most of the situation. Coffee. That was it.

Slipping into her flannel robe and furry slippers, she looked back at Harry, who hadn't moved a muscle since Heather had risen from bed. "Are you coming, or what?"

At that, he jumped down and stretched to his full thirty-six inches, then sauntered down the stairs with Heather following.

****

Heather pulled into Martha's and parked the car in the slot next to Robert's truck. She glanced in the rear view mirror and touched her hand to her wavy red locks. She, smoothed her light coral lipstick on and checked out the results. The voice came again, "what do you really know about him?" She shook her head. "It's only coffee". She grabbed her purse, and opened the door to face the bitter cold.

Heather was greeted by a warm gush of air as she opened the door to Martha's. She saw Martha behind the counter, pouring a cup of coffee and chattering like a magpie to a local fisherman, dressed in a thick corduroy coat and a baseball cap on his head. Heather nodded to her, as she passed the counter.

The weather was keeping the fishermen from going out. Heather saw that each booth in the small diner was full of burly men, all dressed in plaid flannel shirts and jeans, smelling faintly of the sea air.

"Hey, Mike. Are you through at the dock today, or what?"

"No," Mike drew the word out. "Haven't been yet. Need to get some of the nets repaired."

"I hope that you can get it done before it starts snowing again."

Someone from the table next to Mike's offered, "It's not supposed to...at least, not until tonight."

Heather moved past and spotted Robert, alone at a booth in the far corner.

"Hi, there. You look great!" Robert beamed.

As Heather sat down, Martha came to the table to pour them coffee.

"Have you been waiting long?"

"No, not long. Only about ten minutes is all." Robert pushed a menu toward her.

"We agreed on coffee, nothing more." Heather pushed the menu back. She didn't want to give him the advantage. She wanted to be in control.

Robert nudged it back. "What would it hurt to have a pastry with your coffee."

Heather caught herself laughing—she couldn't help herself. Giving in, she glanced over the menu.

Martha came to take their order of two bear claws.

When she retreated, Robert gazed at Heather, who immediately felt like a specimen under a microscope. She squirmed in her seat, and dropped her eyes to her coffee.

"You don't seem like the shy type."

"I'm not." Heather's eyes met his. She told herself to get a grip. "I'm not," she repeated, "but you make me uncomfortable."

"Uncomfortable? I make you…"

"Uncomfortable," she finished his sentence. "You are looking at me as if…I don't know. As if I was from another planet."

Robert laughed. When Heather didn't return his laugh, his smile faded. He cleared his throat. "I certainly didn't mean to make you feel that way, Heather. It's just that…well, I think that you are so beautiful and I feel lucky to be here with you."

Heather's freckled face reddened. She felt relieved when Martha came with two heated bear claws with a glob of butter on each, and refilled their cups.

"Robert, thank you for the compliment, but we don't even know each other. How do you know if you're lucky or not to be with me? I may be a maniacal killer."

Robert guffawed. "You? Not likely. You have as much of a chance of being a killer as me."

Wanting to change the subject, Heather asked, "What do you do for a living, Robert?"

"I'm a nurse. In fact, I…"

Heather nodded her head and finished his sentence. "…took care of Lynn. That's right. I'm not thinking straight, with everything that's going on."

"Maybe you need a break. Have you been to the White Sands yet?"

"No. I've gone to The Twilight, but not The White Sands."

"You should go. I'd love to take you. You'd really like it. The view is spectacular. It's a very classy place. Especially for around here."

"What do you mean by that?"

"It's just that this town is so small. It's a fishing village, for goodness sake!"

"So?" Heather inquired.

"Well, I mean it's not like New York," Robert explained.

The conversation was cut off abruptly when Martha brought more coffee. Robert waited until she was out of earshot before he continued.

Heather cocked her head, as if to question him. "I mean, New York is a city with hundreds of great restaurants, theaters, museums…"

"Crime, smog, garbage, homeless, beggars…" Heather finished Robert's sentence.

Robert laughing, raised his hand to stop Heather bantering. "Okay, okay. I take your point, but I find the city life much more exciting than here, don't you?"

"I can hardly answer that as I haven't lived here; at least, not very long. My boxes of things from the condo in New York came just yesterday, and I haven't even unpacked them. From what I've seen so far, the town is more like a nice, quiet hovel, with the exception of the murder and Nikki being thrown in jail as the number one suspect. The few people that I have met I like."

"Including me?" Robert smiled impishly.

"Of course, including you. Would I be here having coffee and a bear claw if I didn't like you?

"I just wanted to hear you say it." Robert seemed satisfied.

Heather laughed. "Oh, so you are just needy, is that it?"

This time there was no response from Robert, just a hearty laugh. The good natured ridicule was over.

Heather finished her pastry and drained the last of her coffee. With her hand on the strap of her purse, she smiled at Robert and began scooting out of the booth.

"You're not going, are you?"

"I need to get an article in to the magazine by 4:00 this afternoon. Thank you for the coffee. I'll see you later."

"Wait, Heather. I wanted to ask…I want to take you out to dinner. Maybe tonight?"

"Oh, Robert. Tonight wouldn't work. Like I said, I need to work, and afterwords, unpack some boxes. Besides, it's my turn to cook. Thank you for the thought, though. Maybe another night."

"Tomorrow night?"

"I don't know." She was getting testy and, she saw by the look on Robert's face, it showed. She said softer, "Call me tomorrow. I'll have a better idea of what's going on. For now, I need to leave."

They said their goodbyes.

****

After a long night of crying, Nikki was exhausted. She was in the kitchen reading the paper and drinking her morning cup of double dutch coffee. She was glad for the solitary time that Heather had unknowingly given to her. Nikki knew that Heather was having second thoughts about having coffee with Robert—so did Nikki, for that matter; but it was only coffee. What could happen?

It was Christmas week and Heather insisted that they finish decorating the house. Aunt Lynn had started to put up things a few days before she died. Heather said that they should finish the job in honor of her. The only thing that was left was to decorate the tree they had bought the day before. Aunt Lynn had the old family decorations somewhere. It was Nikki's job to find them today while Heather was out with Robert.

Harry walked in, sat at her feet and let out a loud meow. Nikki looked down, and responded, "Yeah, I don't see what she sees in him either, but he is helping to find the killer."

He answered her with an even louder meow.

"Insistent little fellow aren't you?"

Nikki slowly rose from her seat and strolled over the cupboard that held Harry's treats and took several from the bags and dropped them in Harry's dish. Nikki watched as he sauntered over to them, then pointedly sniffed them and walked away.

"Okay. What was that all about? You love your salmon treats. Heather bought them especially for you this time."

He stopped, turned his head and meowed over his shoulder at her, then continued his trek out of the kitchen.

Nikki shook her head and muttered, "Cats!"

Nikki could no longer put off the task at hand; she needed to find the decorations before Heather returned. She dragged herself up the stairs. Suddenly, she was aware of just how creepy the house was when she was the only one in it. Well that was, other than Harry. Harry. He was an enigma to her. He seemed to know just what she was thinking or what she needed, sometimes even before she did. Like right now.

When Nikki reached the attic and opened the door, he was right in front of the bookcase, waiting for her. Wait. How could he be inside when the door was closed?

"How did you...?"

Nikki heard the door squeak and then close itself. That must have been what happened. Heather had to have left the door open last night when she came up here and it closed after Harry got in.

She sighed a sigh of relief. "Good. At least I'm not losing my mind!"

Harry looked up innocently at her and trilled his response.

Nikki bent to scratch behind Harry's ear. He leaned into her nails and closed his eyes, lost in cat heaven.

"Now, where are those ornaments?"

As if she was asking Harry and expecting an answer, he got up and walked casually to a storage closet behind a decorative screen. Harry raised one gigantic paw and touched it to the door, as if pointing.

"In here? Okay." Nikki laughed as she pulled the door open. She stopped dead in her tracks when she saw a half a dozen boxes marked 'Christmas Decorations' in big, black letters. She shook her head in disbelief. "You are creepin' me out, cat!"

Harry meowed and looked at Nikki as though he was pleased with himself, and then ran down the stairs toward the kitchen. Nikki smiled as she descended the stairs behind him and put the boxes in the living room.

Nikki started to open boxes. Some of the tree ornaments that she found, were ones from her childhood. She remembered the first time she "helped" her mom decorate the tree. Now, she examined each one through tears. She felt an emptiness inside as she remembered the accident that took both her mother and her father away from her.

Nikki wiped the tears from her eyes and began to look for hooks to hang the ornaments on the tree.

"Oh, nuts," she said out loud when she couldn't find them. Nikki hurried up stairs, stepped into her boots.

****

Heather ran from her car to the front door of the Victorian. She slipped her key into the lock and burst in the front hall. As she shrugged off her coat, Nikki came downstairs.

"Hey!" Nikki wrapped her scarf and put on her jacket.

"Where are you going?"

"Oh, I couldn't find the hangers for the tree ornaments. I need to run and get some."

"Okay. I'll start my world famous chili while you're gone."

Nikki smiled, grabbed the car keys and her purse. "Great! I'll be back soon."

Heather took out the beans that were soaking overnight and started adding everything but the kitchen sink to the pot. Finally, she stirred in her secret ingredient, peanut butter. Heather smiled when she thought of how everyone, including Nikki, would try to guess what it was that was so different about her chili. Heather had learned how to make it from her grandmother when she was ten years old. She usually added avocado, an ingredient that makes it her own, but they were not in season.

Heather tasted it to make sure that it was perfect.

Satisfied, Heather went to change into her favorite sweats, which were as all sweats such be, baggy and warm. She pulled her wavy red hair into a loose bun at the nape of her neck and held it in place with a clip.

In her office, she resisted the urge to unpack all of the boxes that were stacked up against the far wall.

Heather, instead, sat in front of her computer and stared at the blank screen. This was the worst part of being a writer. Trying to produce a germ of an idea from nothing is like trying to pull teeth without Novocaine, painful and darned near impossible. Especially when her mind has so many things on it. Lynn's death, Nikki getting arrested and being the only suspect so far, trying to find the real killer and Robert. No matter how much she tried not to, Heather really liked him.

Robert was so warm and caring. He also was fun to be with, easy to talk to, and it didn't hurt that he was good looking.

Nikki kept telling her after every break up that Heather went through that she had lousy taste in men, and up until now she would have to agree with Nikki; but this time seemed different. Robert was sincere, and what's more, he acted like an adult, for the most part.

The men in her past either acted like children or were controlling, both of which were deal breakers. Heather expected her men to be trustworthy, respectful, kind, compassionate and grown up. She would not stand for someone that tried to control her every move. She had enough of that growing up. Heather would never forget the way her father treated her mother and vowed that it would never happen to her.

Oh well, she thought, that doesn't matter now, it's in the past. The article that was due at 4:00 p.m. this afternoon was her priority. When Heather started her career in writing, someone gave her a tip for writer's block and she employed it. She began typing what came to mind, no matter if it had to do with the article or not. Soon, her mind focused on the topic of the article and, in an hour, she had finished.

Heather read over the first draft once and was on the second time through, when she heard the front door shut.

"Nikki? Is that you?"

Heather heard footsteps coming down the hall.

"Who else would it be?"

Nikki was standing in the doorway, looking windswept and exhausted. Her beautiful blue eyes were swollen and dull. She obviously had been crying, which had made her mascara run, making her already dark bags under her eyes black, as if someone had given her two black eyes. Normally, she wouldn't have a hair out place, but today her shiny blond mane was frizzy and unkempt.

"What's wrong? Where have you been? You said you would be back soon. That was more than an hour ago."

Nikki plopped herself down into the nearest seat and put her head on her knees.

"I just wish this whole thing would be over. I went to Martha's for a cup of hot chocolate."

"Why go there? We have cocoa here," Heather said.

"I know. I just wanted to be by myself to think."

Heather looked crushed.

Quickly, Nikki added, "Oh no. It's not you. That came out wrong. It's just that I was going through the decorations and it brought back memories of Mom and Dad, which brought back memories of the accident."

"Oh gosh, Nikki. I'm sorry. When I suggested that you do that today, I didn't even think about..."

Nikki held her hand up. "It's okay. Anyway, guess who I ran into at Martha's?"

"Who?"

"O'Neil. That pig of a man strutted over to me and he made sure that everyone in the place could hear him dressing me down like a common criminal. When he left the diner, everyone was either trying not to let on that they heard, or they stared at me as if everything that O'Neil said to me was true."

"So, what did you do?" Heather asked.

"I was going to leave when Martha rushed over, took my arm and led me to the back. She fixed my chocolate and let me cry on her shoulder, while Miranda took over on the floor."

"It sounds like you have had a rough day. Why don't you go up and change out of those wet clothes? Maybe even take a nice hot bath, and I'll pour some wine and make up a plate of goodies." Heather suggested.

"Okay. A bath does sound good."

"Good. Take your time. Your wine will be waiting for you."

*＊＊＊＊＊＊＊

Nikki emerged in an old pair of jeans and an oversized sweatshirt from the University of New England. Her face was scrubbed free of makeup. She had put some eye drops in. She still had bags under her eyes, but at least they weren't swollen anymore.

At the bottom of the stairs, Nikki was met by a mewing Harry.

"What's the matter? Are you hungry?" Nikki asked him.

Harry followed Nikki into the kitchen and sat at attention by the Magic Cupboard. Nikki mixed some wet and dry food together in his dish and put it on the floor. Harry leaped over to the bowl and started to gulp it down without chewing. Nikki leaned against the counter with her arms crossed, watching him devour his food like they never feed him.

Heather rushed in and Nikki's smile vanished.

"What is it, Heather?"

"You are not going to believe this, and I don't want to scare you, but the jerk called again. This time he called my cell."

"What?! How did he get your cell?" Nikki sank into a kitchen chair.

"I don't know. Obviously, it's someone we know."

"Do you use a code on your phone for security?"

"No. I hate taking the time to unlock the blasted thing whenever I want to make a phone call," Heather said.

"Maybe he followed you and I don't know, took it out and copied your home number down."

"When could he have done that? My purse is with me all the time." Heather was confused. She was sure she didn't leave it somewhere where the jerk could get to it.

There was a heavy silence and it was broken when Nikki spoke. "No. Wait a minute. Remember the night we went to dinner at The Twilight? You left your purse in the lounge."

"Oh yeah, but it was only a few minutes before I returned to get it."

"Heather. It only takes a second, if he knows what he is looking for and where he can find it. If it wasn't locked all he would have to do is hit contacts and your number is right on top."

"Okay. I see how he did it, but now what do I do about it"

"You can block the caller," Nikki suggested.

"Then all he has to do is use another phone. No, the only thing to do is change my number. It's too late now. The business office at the phone company is closed."

"I suggest you do it first thing."

Heather said, "I hope he didn't get your number."

"If he did, don't you think he would have called me instead of you?"

"Yeah, I guess so. Anyway, since we can't do a thing tonight, I suggest we go and relax. Our wine and a plate of yummy cheese and crackers are in there." Heather led the way into the living room, where a crackling fire warmed the room.

Heather tuned the stereo to a classical station, while Nikki sunk back into the sofa, put her feet up on the table and closed her eyes, letting the music wash over them until Harry came in to join them, meowing incessantly. The doorbell rang. "You don't suppose that Harry knew there was someone at the door, do you?"

Nikki laughed. "Of course not. Answer the door." She slowly sat up, pulling her feet off of the table and ran her fingers through her hair.

Heather came back into the room with Greg in tow. "Look who's here. It's Deputy Holloway, who just decided to check in on you."

"I'm not on duty now. I'm just Greg."

Greg showed his smile and Nikki couldn't help but melt inside. His smile really got to her, and even though she had sworn off men, Greg could make her forget the heartache that David gave her. She started to think of her ex-fiance and how he left her at the altar. Nikki shook her head to run those thoughts out of her mind.

That was in the past. Nikki looked at Greg. Greg was here now and even though they didn't have anything going on romantically, they were still friends and she needed all of the friends she could get.

Nikki moved over and patted the couch. "Do you want to sit down?"

"Sure," and he sat so close that you could barely get a piece of paper between them. Then he gave her a playful bump.

Nikki smiled. She felt a warm glow inside her. *Greg's just a friend, no more*, she reminded herself.

"So, how are you doing?" Greg asked, as he sat back and stretched his arms on the back of the couch.

"Your timing is great. We just received another call, only this one was on my cell." Heather said.

"What! Okay, it sounds like this guy won't stop until he gets what he is after. Nikki, don't you have any idea what he wants?"

Nikki shook her head vehemently. "No. Unless he is under the impression that the old legend about the Pink Diamond is true."

"That could make a man crazy to get it. At least a greedy man would," Greg said.

"But why wait so long? Why didn't someone else try to get it before this?"

"How do you know that no one has? If someone was willing to kill Lynn for it, couldn't the same thing have happened in the past? Maybe even another Johnson," Heather chimed in.

"Heather, it's just a story. Most people thought that Uncle Frank brought it home from an archeological dig. A few people in town think that he won it from a friend in a high-stakes poker game. Either way, the story is that he came home and hid it somewhere either inside the home or on the property outside without telling anyone where it was before he died."

Greg swallowed a cracker with cheese on it and said, "Another story is that it was a part of a collection that a billionaire owned, and he stole it at a benefit auction. It was to be auctioned off and the starting bid was 90 million dollars. Frank had a reputation of a crazy man, willing to do anything for a buck."

"So, either way, Uncle Frank was crazy," Nikki said.

"Crazy in some ways, like stealing it in the first place right from under armed guards, if that was truly the way he got it, but hiding it was not so crazy as it was smart. It's just too bad he died before he told anybody his secret."

"Obviously, this guy that's harassing us doesn't know that part of the story. Maybe he thinks that we know where it is." Heather reached for another cracker. "Maybe that's a clue?"

"What clue?" Nikki asked.

"Since the guy that's doing all of this, seems to believe that the family knows where the diamond is, maybe that means he's either someone from out of town, or someone who just moved here and heard the story up to the point of him hiding it," Heather explained.

"That's possible." Greg said doubtfully.

"That's just as probable as anything else that we have come up with," Heather retorted.

"Okay, say that we went with that explanation, who is relatively new in town?" Nikki asked.

"What about Roxey? She could be working with some guy, having him make the phone calls." Heather popped a cracker with a slice of cheese into her mouth. "No. It can't be her. She's from here, right?" Heather asked.

"Yeah. Originally. Then, when her mother died when she was five, she was sent to live with her aunt." Nikki followed the cracker with a sip of wine.

"Okay, so why is she back here?"

"She left her aunt's house to live in New York with her boyfriend. When he disappeared with all of Roxey's money, she couldn't afford to continue living there, so she came home to live with her dad. She says that as soon as she gets the money, she's going to get as far away from Harrot Reef as possible," Nikki said.

"Right there we have a motive," Heather said brightly.

"I can't think of anyone else, Nikki. That doesn't mean that there isn't anyone, though. The guy could be from anywhere in the area. Miller's Cove, for instance," Greg said thoughtfully.

Heather sat forward, and grabbed a piece of cheese off of the plate. "What about Roxey's boyfriend? What if Roxey made up with him, or what if they cooked up a scheme to let people think that Roxey was out of his life. She moves back here and starts to plan something. Nobody knows what he looks like, so the boyfriend can move freely around the town. No one would think anything of Roxey going around with the new guy in town."

Greg thought about this scenario. "Okay. It's possible."

"It's better than having Nikki arrested and put in prison for the rest of her life." Heather said. "Okay. We have a suspect, or suspects, we have a motive, Roxey wants to get the money and get out of here and the boyfriend is just greedy. Do we have opportunity, though?"

"Aunt Lynn was always on Roxey's side. She always defended her if someone talked about her in front of Aunt Lynn. I know for a fact, Roxey came over and visited more than a few times," Nikki argued.

Heather pointed out, "She could gain Lynn's trust, sneak the extra arsenic in the tea and get out of there without anyone noticing."

"It sounds plausible. I'll run it by the sheriff tomorrow." Greg stood and stretched his arms over his head. "Okay. I'll call you as soon as I talk to the sheriff tomorrow morning.

Heather walked Greg to the door.

"Watch over her, Heather."

"I always do."

Heather locked and bolted the front door. She turned and leaned on it. She closed her eyes and tried to clear her mind.

"Heather? Are you ready for dinner?"

Heather opened her eyes to the same old world with the same old problems. How are we supposed to get rid of this maniac? She pushed herself away from the door.

Walking into the kitchen, she saw that Nikki was getting down some bowls for the chili.

"Here. Go sit down. I'll get it and bring it to the table," Heather said.

"Okay. What do you want to drink?"

"Water. This chili shouldn't be too hot, but just in case."

They were enjoying a nice, peaceful dinner, both agreeing to talk about anything other than what was going on, when Heather's phone rang again.

They exchanged looks of fear, while Heather pick up the cell and read the display. "Caller Unknown". She muttered to herself as she stabbed at the "Talk" button.

She listened, without saying a word.

"Heather?" It was Greg on the line.

She let out a sigh of relief. "Oh, Greg, it's you."

"Who else…has he called again?"

"No. What's up?"

"Nothing much. I just wanted to let you know that I've looked into the guy that took Roxey for all of her money in New York."

"Yeah? What did you find out?" Heather said with a touch of hope in her voice.

"Just that his name is Conner Dean and the address that we have is bogus."

"Where does it say he lives?"

"In New Jersey, but who knows? The guy could be out of the country by now."

"Was it that much money?" Heather asked incredulously.

"Enough to take the chance of getting caught and going to jail."

"I don't understand, though. If her father owns a deli, I mean, it can't be that much, can it?"

"Exactly what I thought. So I checked into it. Seems that Roxey's dad is really her step-dad. When her mom died, she left Roxey two million dollars. When Roxey received it, she left town and bought a penthouse suite in New York," Greg explained.

"Roxey? In a penthouse? I can't picture her in a penthouse suite."

Up until then, Nikki had been silently listening. This last statement caused her eyes to open wide with surprise. "What!"

Heather covered the mouthpiece on the receiver and mouthed, "I'll tell you when we get through."

Nikki grabbed the phone from Heather, and in a loud voice, "Greg? What's this about Roxey and a penthouse? She's barely twenty one."

"Okay, look. I'll explain when I see you tomorrow."

"Oh, no you don't. Now. I want to know what this has to do with my aunt's death. You wouldn't have bothered calling if you didn't think it was important."

"Nikki, I didn't mean to upset you, it's just that I found out some information that could have something to do with all of this. If Roxey had that much money at her disposal, and this guy stole it from her, I'm just wondering what she wouldn't do to get her hands on that kind of money now."

"What does that have to do the Aunt Lynn?"

"Don't you see, Nikki? Your family has money. She might have tried to get it from your aunt, and in the process, killed her," Greg said.

"Okay, You have got a point. But why would she do it?"

"She doesn't have to have a reason except that she wants money."

"Aunt Lynn treated her like her own daughter. I just can't believe that Roxey would do this."

"There is nothing tying her to it, at least not for now. It's just a lead. A small one to be sure, but a lead just the same," Greg said.

There was silence on the line.

"Nikki? You still there?

"Yeah. What now?"

"What do you mean?"

"I mean, what will you do now?"

""I will bring this latest information to Grady, er, I mean, the sheriff."

"Like he'll do something with it," Nikki scoffed.

"No, I think that he might be interested in this theory. And Nikki...that's all it is at this point, a theory. Now, you relax tonight, get a good night's sleep. I'll see you at breakfast."

"Martha's?"

"Where else?"

Chapter 17

Friday, December 21st

Nikki woke to the ringing of the phone on her night table. Sleepily, she answered it. "Hello?"

There it was. That raspy breathing. Only this time, before she could think what to do, she heard:

"Give it to me or you'll end up like your aunt."

Her heart was in her throat. She pulled herself into a sitting position. She was shaking and felt her pulse racing, she yelled into the phone,

"Give what to you?"

"Give it to me" he repeated. "Or you'll end up like your aunt." Then he was gone. All that she heard was a dial tone.

Heather raced into the room. "Nikki, what's wrong? You look like you've seen a ghost. Was that him? What did he say?"

"The same thing that he always says. 'Give it to me'. Only this time he added or I'll end up like my aunt."

Heather stared at Nikki for a second, then said, "Are you okay?"

Nikki nodded, threw the sheets back and slowly got out of bed. "I don't know if I'm scared or just angry."

"Well, it's better to be angry. Approach this whole thing with a clear head and some coffee. I just made some."

Nikki smiled. "I'll be down in a minute. I need to throw something on if we're meeting Greg today."

Nikki crawled out from under the sheets, glanced in the full length mirror next to dressing table. She pulled a face at her reflection, then turned to go get showered. She emerged wearing designer jeans and a pink mohair sweater. Her long, blond hair was still damp and curly. She had a minimum amount of makeup on; just enough to hide the fact that she had very little sleep.

"You feel better?" Heather handed Nikki a steamy hot cup of mocha espresso.

"Yeah, I guess so. What is going on with all of these phone calls, the email, the letter and the roses? I just can't think of who would send them and why."

"I don't know," Heather answered simply.

"Last night, he said 'Give it to me.' This morning he said 'Give it to me or you'll end up like your aunt.' It could be anyone. It's a small town and everyone knows that Aunt Lynn is dead."

"We will figure it out. Greg called while you were in the shower. He and Robert are meeting us over here instead of Martha's," Heather said.

Nikki took a bagel out of the toaster oven and was spreading cream cheese on it. When she heard that Robert was coming with Greg, Nikki stopped and looked quizzically up at Heather, who had turned to leave the room.

"Robert is coming, too? Why?"

"I don't know. I guess that he just wants to help out."

Heather slowly walked back in the kitchen with the newspaper. Nikki was nibbling on her bagel, when she saw the alarmed look on Heather's face. She dropped her bagel on the plate.

"What?" When Heather didn't answer. "Heather, what?"

Heather tore the rubber band off the paper and handed her a note. The paper that it was written on was the same as what the letter was written on. Nikki immediately felt sick to her stomach. She took it from Heather with a shaky hand and read it.

"Where is it?"

It was simple, yet effective.

"What does this guy want." Nikki eyes welled up with tears. "What could Aunt Lynn have had that he killed her for?"

"Now, it's pretty clear that she was murdered. The note is written proof of harassment, at least."

"O'Neil will say that I wrote it to throw him off track. Besides, it's in block letters and could be written by anyone, which is why he did it that way," Nikki argued.

"You know, I wonder if it could be him."

"Who? O'Neil? Heather, he's the sheriff."

"Yeah, but he has had it out for your family for years. You said so yourself. He could be framing you, couldn't he?"

"Why would he risk his job to kill Aunt Lynn and harass me? I mean, he's a jerk, but to kill someone? No, I don't think so."

"Well, he's still on *my* list of suspects. I just don't trust that man. How did he get to be sheriff anyway?" Heather asked.

"He promised that he would make this town more prosperous."

"And has he?"

"No. He's made it worse. Half the town knows he's dirty, but they can't prove it."

"What about the other half? What do they think?"

"They're all good ol' boys who stand beside him no matter what. Of course, they do this for a price. That's how he keeps the position. The good ol' boys. Do I think he is capable of framing me for this? Yes. Do I think he would risk getting caught and end up in the position where even his dirty pals can't do anything? No. He likes the power too much to take the chance of losing it."

Their conversation was interrupted by the doorbell.

Heather opened the door to see Greg and Robert on the porch.

"Hey, guys." Heather took a couple of steps back to let them in.

"We're in the kitchen. Do you want some coffee?" Heather offered.

"Yeah, please," they replied in unison.

"Nikki, are you okay?" Greg said as soon as he lay eyes upon her. He could tell, even under the makeup she wore to hide the fact she had little sleep, something was drastically wrong.

No matter how much she tried, she couldn't keep the tears from welling up in her eyes.

"Nikki?" Greg went to her and tenderly took her by the shoulders. "What happened?"

Nikki shook her head then turned away, looking at Heather with pleading eyes.

"She's had a couple of scares this morning. First, he called again."

Heather repeated the conversation between Nikki and 'The Jerk', as they started to call him.

"Then there was this on our newspaper this morning." Heather held up the note.

Greg read the threatening note and shook his head. "What time did you pick up the newspaper?"

"I don't know. About 20 minutes to a half hour ago."

"And when does your paper come?"

"Gosh, I'm not sure. Since we've been here, it comes 8:00 maybe 8:30, unless it snows. Then they have to wait until the roads are clear. On those days it could be as late as noon. It's clear today and, apparently, didn't snow during the night, so it probably came around 8:00 - 8:30" Heather was more or less talking to herself, trying to calculate, so as to be as accurate as possible.

"So, it's probably somebody nearby."

Greg turned away from Heather. Did you figure out what he's after yet, Nikki?"

"No. Except…" Nikki broke off. "What if it's the diamond that they're after?"

"What diamond?" This time it was Robert who spoke.

"Well," she started off slowly. "There is a story about my great-uncle bringing back a rare diamond."

"So, if it were true, where would it be?" Robert's eyes were flashing with excitement.

Nikki started to have the same feeling again. That feeling that Robert wasn't exactly what he seemed. Nikki immediately closed up.

"I think it was just a story that my great uncle made up. It's nothing. Forget it."

"What if it's true?" Robert said.

"Forget it, Robert. If Nikki says that it's not true, then we need to think of something else that he may have been referring to." To Nikki and Heather, Greg asked, "Have you had breakfast today?"

"Kinda late for breakfast, isn't it?" Heather smiled .

"Okay, brunch then."

"Nikki. Are you hungry?"

Nikki was lost in thought, but when she heard her name, she came out of her reverie. "Yeah, as a matter of fact, I am."

"Well, then. Grab your coats. We will have to meet you there because we came in Robert's truck."

****

After brunch, Nikki and Heather were walking up the walkway to the manor, when they heard the phone ringing.

Nikki ran ahead, careful not to slip on the ice, and grabbed the phone . Heather came in behind her and shrugged off her jacket.

"Hello?" Nothing. "Hello? Who is this?" Nikki's voice became shaky. "Hello?"

The next thing Nikki heard was someone breathing into the phone. "Guess."

Nikki slammed down the phone.

"Who was that?" Heather wanted to know, as if she didn't know already.

"I don't know. Someone was breathing into the phone like..."

"A prank call, Nikki. That's all it was," Heather assured her.

The phone rang again. Heather answered and again heard nothing but heavy breathing.

"Listen, jerk. I don't know who you are, and frankly I don't care. If you are trying to scare us, forget it. I've heard worse from sickos like you." Heather slammed the receiver down on the base."

"Do you think that was smart, Heather?"

"Why? You need to show that you are not afraid of jerks like that. He's probably some nut who heard what was going on with us. Maybe it's some kids trying to get their kicks."

"Yeah. I guess you're right."

The doorbell rang and Nikki nearly jumped out of her skin. Heather signaled for her to sit back down. "Relax. I'll get it."

She came back in with an arrangement of roses painted black.

"Who sent those?" Nikki hurried over to Heather.

"I don't know. There isn't a card."

"Okay, this is getting spooky. First, they send roses that are dead the other day, and now I get a bouquet painted black."

"Nikki, what did I just tell you? They are just trying to scare us."

"But why?"

"That's what we have to find out. Let's call Greg."

Heather pulled her cell from her back pocket and dialed the Sheriff's Office number. When O'Neil answered in his gruff voice, she couldn't help but to roll her eyes and mumble "Oh, no."

"Sheriff. This is Heather Murphy, Nikki Johnson's friend."

"Yeah, I remember you." He spat the words out as though they were a bad taste in his mouth. "What's wrong now?"

She couldn't believe how horrible this man was. He couldn't be more unpleasant if he tried. "Nikki has been receiving some phone calls today…"

Sighing heavily. "So? Did anyone get hurt?"

"Well…no, but…"

"Do you know who it was?"

"No, but…"

"Then what do you expect us to do about it? If you don't even know who is making the calls, how do you expect us to follow up on it? You know, we are not here to hold Miss Johnson's hand when something happens. Now, I've got real work to do."

Heather stood there listening to a dial tone.

"Okay, so that was a mistake. Let's call Greg on his cell phone. You have his number?"

Nikki rifled through her handbag and came up with a phone number on a piece of paper. "(207) 555-2359."

Heather heard the phone ringing once and it was picked up by Greg.

"Hello?"

"Greg? This is Heather."

"Hi Heather. What's up?"

"Well, we have had some problems."

"What kind of problems? Is Nikki okay?"

"Yes she's okay, but she's a little shaken."

"Why?"

"We have had a few phone calls since we came home from Martha's this afternoon."

"What kind of phone calls?"

"Well, nothing threatening. Just some heavy breathing. Nikki answered the first phone call, got no response and she hung up. Then they called right back and I took it and I gave them an earful."

"So they didn't speak to you at all? You don't know if it was a man or a woman?"

"No. They didn't talk they just breathed heavy. And whispered. We couldn't tell anything. I told Nikki that it was a possibility it's just kids."

"Yeah, you're probably right, but let me know if it happens again."

"We called O'Neil but he was his usual charming self and wrote it off as a nuisance call and hung up on me."

"Yeah well, that sounds like him. Next time that something like this comes up, just call my cell. We will keep O'Neil out of it as much as possible."

"There's something else, Greg. Right after the phone calls, the doorbell rang. When I answered it, there was nobody there but whoever rang the doorbell left a bunch of black roses. I tried to tell O'Neil about it, but he hung up before I could get it out of my mouth."

"Why doesn't that surprise me?" There was a silence on the line, and then Greg spoke out. "Black roses, eh? I don't think the florist here in town carries them. I know they're a Gothic specialty. Roxey had some delivered to her at the bakery from her boyfriend. Maybe she would know where he got them."

"Yeah, that sounds like a good idea. Can you let us know after you talk to her?"

"Sure. You have a cell phone, right?"

"Yeah, why?" Heather asked.

"You know how you can buy different ringtones? I want you to get one that is loud and annoying, like a whistle or a horn. Now, if he calls again, instead of giving him the satisfaction of showing anger or fear, I want to play that in the mouthpiece. You got it?"

"Yeah, that's a good idea. Why didn't I think of that? Thanks, Greg. We really appreciate your help."

"Sure. You know I'm here to help you guys. You and Nikki take it easy tonight and I will come by to check on you in the morning."

Chapter 18

Saturday, December 22nd

The next day was gloomy. There was a storm coming in, and the radio said that it was going to be a bad one. "Batten down the hatches."

Nikki and Heather were going over the last minute details for tomorrow's memorial service.

"Hey look, Heather."

Nikki walked into the kitchen with a giant, red heart candy box.

"Is there a card this time?"

"Yeah. It's from Greg. It says 'I hope you have a sweet Christmas. Love, Greg.' "

"Kind of sappy for Greg, don't you think? Are you sure it's from him?"

"Heather, it says right here on the card. See?"

"Yeah, but…"

"I'll just put it in the living room while we eat our lunch."

Nikki put the unopened box of candy on the coffee table, petted Harry and went into the kitchen to eat lunch.

When Nikki and Heather returned, the candy was all over the floor. Each piece was smashed with big paw prints. Harry sat in the corner, quietly bathing.

"What the…?" Nikki said.

Heather picked a piece of the candy up and smelled it.

"It smells strange. Like almonds."

"Maybe that's an almond one."

Nikki smelled another.

"I don't smell anything."

"Here. Let me see that one." Heather sniffed. "It smells the same as the others. Are you sure you can't smell anything?"

"Nothing but chocolate."

"Nikki, I think these have been tampered with."

"But I don't smell anything," Nikki insisted.

"I know, but I read somewhere that not everyone can smell cyanide, which smells like bitter almonds. The question is, why would "The Jerk" change MO's now? Why cyanide and not arsenic?"

"Maybe he used arsenic on Lynn because he knew that the chances of detection were slim to none. The doctor told me that the tea has a strong odor and it doesn't hurt that it has a trace of arsenic in it."

"Yeah, and the chances of us...I mean you eating the chocolate that has an almond smell, bitter or not, are far more likely than if you smelled garlic."

"Maybe that explains why Harry didn't stop Aunt Lynn from drinking tea that has poison in it. Maybe he couldn't smell it either."

"I don't know, but let's ask Greg if he sent them, just in case. If not, we'll know that "The Jerk" is cranking it up a notch."

They gathered all of the candy into the broken box that Harry gnawed open.

"If they're poisoned, I wonder how it is that Harry's not sick or worse?"

"He obviously didn't eat any of it," Nikki said.

Heather called Greg's private number. She told him about the candy and how the card said they were from him. After a short conversation, Heather hung up the phone. She sat down next to Nikki on the brocade couch in the living room..

"Greg didn't send them. He says that he'll be right over to pick them up. He'll request that they be tested, but it probably won't get done until after Christmas."

Chapter 19

Sunday, December 23th

Nikki was in the bathroom, adding the last touches to her makeup. She was hit, once again, with the fact that Lynn was gone, and Nikki would never see her again. She looked in the mirror and saw a sad, broken woman staring back at her. She tried to console herself with the thought that she still had Heather, who stood beside her through thick and thin, but Heather wasn't blood. She wasn't really family, although she was like a sister to Nikki. It was contradictory, she knew. If she had Heather, who was like a sister, then why should she feel so alone. Nikki should feel that she still had *family*.

Her head was still spinning with these thoughts, when she heard a gentle rap on the door.

"Nikki, are you okay in there?" Heather asked, her voice laced with concern.

Nikki shook loose the thoughts that had taken over her mind. "Yeah, Heather. I'll be out in a minute."

"Okay."

It wasn't until she heard Heather's retreating footsteps, that Nikki's body started to shake uncontrollably. She gripped the counter in front of her. Her knees were like jelly. She felt her heart pounding. Even though she became hot from the inside out, she broke out into a cold sweat. She knew that she was going to get sick seconds before it happened. All that she could think of was *"thank God I'm not in my new dress"*.

Nikki washed her face. She had to start all over, applying makeup and styling her hair. Then she would don her new dress. It was a ruby red classic sleeveless dress with a matching jacket. Nikki was lucky to find something so elegant here. They had to go to Greendale, just on the outskirts of the county border, and the nearest city with a mall in it. The last thing she put on was her aunt's single strand of pearls. She stepped back to look at herself. *Well, that'll have to be good enough.*

When Nikki reached the bottom of the stairs, she was lost in a sea of activity. The caterers were setting up long tables in the dining room while the florist was filling each room with floral arrangements.

The doorbell rang and Heather went to answer it, but Harry was stretched out in front of the door.

"Harry. Must you always be in the way?"

"Trill," was the response that Heather received.

Heather opened the door to find Greg standing on the other side. He was as handsome as ever in his Calvin Klein suit.

"Well, hello handsome."

Greg smiled. He saw Nikki standing at the bottom of the stairs and went to her.

"Are you okay, Nikki?" Greg asked.

Nikki shook her head slightly as if trying to clear her head. "Yeah, I'm fine."

"You do look a little peaked," Heather said. "Why don't you sit down over here..." Heather led her to the living room and indicated a chair by the fireplace, "...and I'll get you some water."

As Nikki sat down, she said in a weak voice, "I'm fine, guys. Really," but Heather had already disappeared into the kitchen.

Greg sat in the matching chair next to Nikki. "Listen. During the service, I want you to keep your eyes and ears open."

"Why?" Heather said, as she walked in with a glass of water for Nikki.

"Because in a small town like this, there's bound to be some gossip flying around. Listen for anything that sounds..." Greg was at a loss for the proper words.

"Hinky?" Heather suggested.

Greg smiled. "Thanks, Heather. Yes, hinky. Especially concerning Stu, Miranda, Rhoda and Roxey. Also, it's not totally unusual for a killer to attend the funeral or memorial service of his or her victims. If you suspect something, don't confront the person yourself. Get me instead and I'll take care of it. By the way, how are you going to get everyone in here?"

"We thought of that. I sent the people who were closest to Aunt Lynn, and of course all the suspects, an announcement stating that the memorial service would start at a certain time, while the time I had put in the paper was an hour later. That way, there would be enough room for the service, and people could come by and pay their respects afterward," Nikki answered.

Nikki noticed that people were starting to arrive. Nikki stood by the door to greet the mourners, while Heather directed them to the living room, where there were folding chairs lined up in front of the fireplace.

When all of the guests were seated, Nikki went and stood by the hearth.

"I want to thank you all for coming today. Years ago, Aunt Lynn shared with me what her wishes were following her death. So, this is the celebration of her life that she requested. I've asked a few people to come and speak about my aunt's life, but first I would like to tell you a little about Aunt Lynn as an aunt, mother, sister and friend, all of which she was to me."

"Most of you know that when I was ten years old, my parents were killed in a hit and run accident. Aunt Lynn came out to California and brought me back here. She raised me as if I was her own daughter, but our relationship had an even closer bond than some mother and daughter relationships because she was the most important person in my world and the only person who I could trust in my life. When I moved to New York, we remained close..." Nikki's tears started to trickle down her cheeks.

Heather stood, gently took her friend's arm and guided her to her chair. She turned toward the group and caught Stu's eye. Heather motioned for him to come up and say a few words.

By the time all of the speeches were done, the townspeople started to arrive.

Greg caught Robert's attention from across the room. Robert excused himself from a conversation to come and join Greg, Nikki, and Heather.

"Like I told the ladies earlier, keep your eyes and ears open as you mingle. We'll get together tomorrow night to discuss each other's findings."

They all agreed.

****

Later that evening, Nikki, Heather, Greg and Robert were sitting in front of the fireplace in the living room, exchanging notes from the ceremony. A blizzard was blowing up a storm and the crackling fire was comforting, as well as warm.

Robert snatched another piece of pepperoni pizza and spread some anchovies on it before he stuffed half of it into his mouth.

Greg took a sip of his root beer. "When I questioned Miranda, she told me that, although Stu didn't want to tell about the affair they were having, she thought it best. According to Miranda, Rhoda was sitting in the diner two days before Lynn died, and she overheard Miranda tell one of her friends that she was meeting Stu at White Sands. When Miranda said, 'And then, who knows what will happen?', both of the girls giggled and lowered their voices so that Rhoda could no longer hear the conversation."

"So," Greg continued, "Rhoda concocted a plan to get Stu away from your aunt. She asked Lynn out to dinner at the White Sands on the same night as when Stu and Miranda were to meet. When they walked in, Rhoda purposely pointed out the table where Stu and Miranda were sitting."

Heather almost choked on her pizza. "What a spiteful thing to do!"

"Yeah, I know. So, anyway, Miranda told me afterward, that Rhoda had this smug look on her face, like she was so pleased that Lynn saw that Stu was cheating on her."

"I still can't believe that Miranda was having an affair with Stu. My gosh, he's old enough to be her father!"

"There's something else that I don't understand." Nikki picked up a piece of pizza and watched as the cheese stretched the further she pulled it from the box. All eyes were on her. "If Stu was a cheat, why would Rhoda want anything to do with him?"

"Beats me." Greg shrugged his shoulders. "Why does Rhoda do anything?"

"Rhoda was obsessed with Stu. Maybe she was one of those women who thinks that she can change a man," Robert added.

Heather slowly nodded in agreement. "So, then what happened?"

Greg went on with his story. "The next night, Stu came over here to try to smooth things out with Lynn. Rhoda was coming over to visit Lynn and, according to her, she could hear them screaming at each other. It only takes a few hours for Rhoda to spread it around town that Stu is cheating on Lynn, and what's worse, it was with sweet, 'girl next door', Miranda. This bit of information shocked everyone, even more that the fact that Stu was stepping out on Lynn."

Heather shook her head. "This is a real soap opera, isn't it?"

"So, Stu is Miranda's alibi for the night that Aunt Lynn was killed," Nikki said.

"That's what our next step is, to check alibis. Stu says that Miranda is lying and that he was out of town, but he can't prove it and, in my experience, that usually means that something fishy is going on."

"Why would Stu want Lynn dead anyway? I could see if it was an accident that happened during the fight, but you can't accidentally poison someone." Heather took a sip of her root beer.

"Okay. Let's put Stu on the back burner. We need to find out more about the fight."

"What about Rhoda? She seems bent on doing anything to get Stu back. Do you think that she would poison Lynn to have Stu to herself again?" Nikki asked.

"It doesn't seem very likely. How many people would kill for love?" Robert asked.

"Oh, come on, Robert. Have you never heard of 'crime of passion'? Especially with someone as 'off' as Rhoda. Plus...she doesn't have much of an alibi...home alone?" Nikki pointed out, as she popped the last bite of her pizza into her mouth licked her finger tips, and started to get up.

"Does anyone else want some more root beer?"

"I'll help." Heather followed her out of the room.

"Okay. Truth." Heather faced Nikki when they were out of earshot. "You like Robert now?"

Nikki smiled. "Like?"

"No, not like that, but you aren't suspicious of him anymore?"

"Okay. Yeah, he's a nice guy and he apparently took very good care of Aunt Lynn. My problem with him at first was that he had the most opportunity."

"What was his motive though?"

"Exactly. Even Greg, who took me quite seriously, checked him out even though Robert is his best friend, and couldn't find a reason for Robert to kill her," Nikki acquiesced.

They took the sodas back into the living room.

"So, Rhoda and Stu are our strongest suspects?" Heather asked.

"Yeah, right now it looks that way." Greg reached for his glass and smiled a silent thanks to Nikki.

"Stu's alibi was that he was out of town, but Miranda said she was with Stu. Someone's obviously lying. Rhoda was home alone," Nikki said.

"Of course," Heather spat.

"What about Roxey? Where does she fit?" Robert asked.

"She's a good suspect too. She's always been greedy, and since she lost all of her inheritance, she has been looking for some way to 'get rich quick'. In walks Lynn. Roxey smells the money and takes advantage of her," Greg agreed.

"Did anyone talk to her yesterday?" Heather asked.

Nikki shook her head. "I know it sounds plausible, but I don't want to believe that Roxey would do anything like killing Aunt Lynn."

Greg smiled and put his hand on Nikki's knee. "That's what I like about you, Nikki. Your ability to see the good in everybody."

"Not everybody." She sneaked a peek at Robert and then shook her head.

Chapter 20

Christmas Eve

It was Christmas Eve and Nikki was up in the attic looking for some stockings to hang on the mantle.

"Oh, Harry! Stop scratching the bookcase! I'll get the ball."

When Nikki shoved the bookcase over, it seemed that Harry had not been after the toy, but instead, he stood on his hind legs and stretched his long body to scratch at the wall. The puzzled Nikki watched the cat scratching wildly at the wall.

"What is it, Harry?"

The cat stopped his pawing and looked up at Nikki with expectancy in his eyes.

"I have no idea what you want?"

Harry started to scratch at the wall again. It was then that Nikki saw a faint, square outline. She pushed the right side of it, and it popped open to reveal a compartment with a small safe inside.

"Wow, a secret compartment! Now how did you know this was here, Harry?" Nikki asked the cat, who just looked at her and then wound himself around her legs, rubbing as he went.

Nikki looked in the compartment and saw a locked safe. "Oh, great." She looked down at Harry. "You wouldn't happen to know the combination, would you?"

Then Nikki remembered the slip of paper with the strange numbers and letters on it.

"That's it," she cried with excitement.

Nikki ran down one flight of stairs to her bedroom. *Now, which pants was I wearing when I found it.* She rifled through her pants until she found the small envelope with the slip of paper inside.

Nikki ran up to the attic and tried the combination. The safe opened. Inside, there was a book. Nothing else, just a book. She pulled it out with shaky hands. Opening it to the first page, she read the year *1815*.

"Wow."

The next page read:

"*If you are reading this book, you are a Johnson.*"

Nikki flipped through the diary to another page.

"*The house was finished yesterday. Last night, a cat came to the door begging to be let in. It was the biggest cat that I have ever seen. The children have named him 'Harry'.*"

"Harry," Nikki mumbled.

Suddenly, Nikki heard footsteps on the stairs. Something told her that she wasn't to share this diary with anyone. Not just yet, anyway. Quickly, she closed the book and threw it in the safe. She was just stuffing the piece of paper with the combination in her back pocket, when Heather stuck her head in.

"Nikki? There you are. I've been looking all over for you." Heather walked in the room. "What are you doing up here?"

"Just looking for the stockings that we used to hang on the mantle."

"Behind the bookcase?"

"Huh? Oh, Harry lost his ball and I was getting it for him."

Nikki picked the ball up and rolled it toward Harry. Harry played his part by pushing it back to Nikki. She looked past Heather and saw the stockings that she wanted on the top of a box.

"There they are." Nikki walked past Heather, grabbed them and started to leave the room. "Are you coming?"

"Yeah. I almost forgot. Greg phoned and told me to tell you that he would be here in a few minutes.."

As if on cue, the doorbell rang. Nikki ran down the stairs and opened the door.

"Hi. Come on in. I'll just be a few more minutes." Nikki turned and went upstairs to her bedroom. There she put the slip of paper with the safe combination on it into the top drawer of her dresser. She looked at herself in the mirror and slipped a stray piece of hair behind her ear.

Heather indicated that Greg should follow her into the living room and sit down while waiting for Nikki. Heather sat across the room from him. "So, where are you guys going?"

"I'm taking her to the White Sands as a surprise."

"Oh, good. She needs to get away from here. She is under a lot of stress, what with her aunt dying and then to find that Lynn was murdered. It's all so horrible. Nikki won't even go into the library."

"That'll change eventually. I think that when the killer is caught and put away, she will feel much more comfortable in this house, for that matter, in the town."

They stopped their conversation when they heard Nikki on the stairs. All eyes were on her, as she breezed into the room.

"You look beautiful, as always." Greg stood, took her arm and gave her a light kiss on her cheek.

As they turned to walk to the door, Nikki called over her shoulder, "Have fun with Robert tonight."

"Robert is taking you out?" asked Greg.

"Well, no. Actually, I invited him over for dinner."

"Oh, a cheap, date, eh?" Greg winked at Heather.

Heather blushed. "Go on. Have a nice dinner."

"We'll see you later."

Greg led Nikki to Robert's truck.

"Why are we taking Robert's truck?" Nikki asked.

"Earlier today, I had engine trouble and had to have my car towed to Marty's Garage. Besides costing double due to it being Christmas Eve, it left me with no car. Robert offered to lend me his truck, with one condition…that I fill the tank before bringing it back," Greg explained.

"How is he getting over here, then?"

"He's got an old Camaro."

"Oh," Nikki said simply. "So, where are we going?"

"White Sands, if that's okay?"

Nikki was lost in her thoughts, as the car slowly maneuvered through the falling snow. She started to wonder what his intentions were. The White Sands was the most romantic place in town. Nikki didn't think of Greg that way, and she hoped that Greg didn't feel that way toward her.

When Greg came to a halt at a stop sign, the truck stalled.

He mumbled under his breath, "I'm not used to driving this darned thing."

Greg got the truck started and turned on Harbor Street. He looked over at Nikki next to him.

"Penny for your thoughts?"

Nikki broke her gaze and turned, smiled at him and responded, "They're not worth that much."

"Let me be the judge."

Nikki shrugged her shoulders uncomfortably. "The truth?"

Greg nodded.

"I was wondering why we were going to The White Sands instead of Martha's or the Twilight?"

"Do we have to have a special reason? I just thought it would be pleasant to have a nice dinner, for a change. Not that Martha's or even the Twilight wouldn't have been good, but I just thought that I... we...needed a nice quiet dinner, just the two of us, and The Sands is quieter than Martha's or The Twilight."

"Hmm."

"What?"

"Just hmm."

As they pulled into the parking lot of the restaurant, the snow stopped falling. They walked along the cobblestone walkway.

"You look very pretty tonight."

Nikki blushed. She needed to remind herself that Greg was only a friend who started out as being a means to an end. Very quickly, their relationship changed to friendship, but only a friendship. Nikki didn't dare let a man get too close to her again.

Greg held open the door and Nikki slipped past him into the warmth of the restaurant. He helped Nikki off with her coat, and then walked to the podium, where the maitre d' waited to greet them.

"Two for Holloway," Greg said.

The maitre d' looked at his book and found Greg's name. "Yes, Sir. If you would come this way, please."

Ironically, they were led to the table where Nikki and Tom sat the last time she came. The time that she had to 'let Tom down easy'. It seems that's all she has done this week…let men down. First Tom, now Greg? She just hoped that she wouldn't have to do it again. Nikki hardly knew Greg and he was a very important person to have helping her find out who killed Aunt Lynn.

Greg asked for a bottle of 1961 Bordeaux.

The maitre'd raised his eyebrows, knowing that 1961 was a very good year for bordeauxs. "Yes, sir. I'll inform your waiter."

Nikki caught Greg gazing at her. She shifted uncomfortably in her seat. Then Greg smiled that sexy smile that made her knees turn to quivering jelly.

"You really do look…" searching for the appropriate words, "nice tonight."

"Thanks."

Nikki opened her menu and looked down—pretending to read it—to try to hide the blush in her cheeks. The waiter came with the bottle of wine, and she regained her composure.

Only after they ordered their dinners, did Greg start to talk about why he brought her here. Nikki was pleasantly surprised when it was not anything on the personal level.

"So, you were right. I found a little shop in San Francisco that sells that tea. One couple bought it, then died because of it."

"The store is still in business after all that?" Nikki sounded astonished.

"Surprisingly, yes. They must know someone who knows someone. So, I asked for the importer. They were reluctant to tell me, until I said the word 'injunction.'"

"Oh? What? Did they give the name to you?"

"Yep. It's a company over in China. Don't ask me what the name of the company is because I couldn't pronounce it if I tried. Anyway, I've faxed them an order for them to give us a list of local shops that bought the tea. I expect to hear from them tomorrow."

"Why couldn't they give you the list today? There can't be that many places."

"Nikki, it will take some time to gather the names up and send them to us."

When she looked disappointed, Greg leaned across the table, touched her hand and in his low, sexy voice, "It will come. Then we will be that much closer to learning who killed Lynn."

Nikki straightened up in her chair, nodded her head and gently pulled her hand away from him. "Then what?"

"*Then what, what?*"

"After you get the list. What will you do with it?"

"What I do best...good old detective work. Don't worry. We'll find out who bought it."

"But what if the buyer paid cash? Or, even worse, what if the person who bought it wasn't the one who put arsenic in it?" Nikki felt herself losing control.

"We have to go under the assumption that the person who bought it is the killer. We aren't worried about the customer paying cash. With a warrant, we can go through receipts. Don't worry, I know what I'm doing."

"Okay. Well, we know that Aunt Lynn was drinking the Pu-erh for her high blood pressure. So, she would buy it anyway. But what I don't get is, if she bought it, and she drank nearly all, well all except the last bit, then why didn't she die sooner?"

"First of all, we don't know if she bought it, do we? And if she did, couldn't it be possible that someone sneaked it in there?" Greg suggested.

"Well, I suppose. She did entertain lot." Nikki wasn't convinced. "I would feel a lot better if I knew just how it happened. O'Neil hasn't been real helpful either."

"That's because he is trying to tie you to this."

"But I didn't..."

Greg cut her off, "I know, Nikki. It's just a matter of proving you didn't and then he'll have to leave you alone. In the meanwhile, let me do my job, please."

****

The Gang was gathering at the fence for one last report. Little Bea was so excited to tell about her mission with Harry. He had told her that she could share it all by herself. This was the first time ever that Harry had confidence in her, just like one of the big cats.

As usual, the ruckus was getting louder.

Harry raised his paw. "Okay, everyone. Let's call this meeting to order."

All of them went silent. Then it happened. Harry heard the roar; felt the shiver down his spine; and somewhere in the distance, he heard "Harry, you're needed right now!" It was his trusted favorite charge, Lynn, coming back to him from the dead.

Harry vanished and reappeared in the front hall of the manor house.

****

Heather pulled free the last ringlet in her long red hair, as she raced down the stairs. The doorbell rang a second time and Harry ambled over and blocked the door.

"Shoo, Harry."

Harry slowly stood, stretched and let out an especially loud meow. Heather bent to scoot him out of the way and opened the door. On the other side stood Robert, wrapped in his brown leather coat with the collar turned up against the cold wind. In his hand were a dozen red roses.

Robert crossed the threshold, kissed Heather on the cheek and gave her the roses. Immediately, the sweet fragrance of the flowers filled her senses.

"Oh, Robert! You shouldn't have, but I'm glad you did. They're beautiful." She brought her face down to the petals and took a long, deep breath. "Thank you."

Robert shrugged off his jacket. He was in jeans and a dark blue polo shirt, which set off his deep blue eyes. Heather took a moment to appreciate his boyish good looks. His reddish-brown waves were wet and droplets of water dripped from tight curls. His impish smile revealed his playful mood.

It wasn't until Robert turned to follow Heather into the formal dining room, that Harry noticed a slight bulge under his shirt. The tingling started again. The roar surrounded him like an ocean tide rushing in and pounding on the beach. There was something wrong. Harry trotted after the humans, trying not to show his concern for Heather. He never trusted Robert when he took care of Lynn. Now, he was overwhelmed with the same sensation he had that horrible night when his charge was killed. This time, however, Harry would be right here to save Heather, if need be; and, from the way he felt, he would be needed.

The table was set for two with Nicki's great grandmother's bone china, crystal, and polished silver. Generations of Johnsons had entertained the most powerful people in the county on these dishes and tonight Nikki was letting Heather use them. Between the silver, dishes and crystal and her scrumptious cooking, she would be sure to impress Robert.

Heather reached for a lighter to light the red, tapered candles. Robert gently took it from her.

"Wait. I'll do that."

The clicking of the shiny gold lighter ignited a flame. Robert held it to the waiting wicks and watched as they flared to life. He snapped the lighter closed and held Heather's chair out for her.

"This dinner looks fantastic," Robert said.

"I hope you like it. It's my grandmother's recipe."

The fragrance of the garlic, onions and herbs, mingled with the dry white wine, came together to make a tempting aroma. Heather could tell from Robert's blissful expression that she had made the Chicken Cacciatore just right. She smiled, then filled her fork with the yummy chicken and sauce. She was relieved to find that it tasted like grandma's...well, almost.

"So, how was your day?" Heather inquired.

Robert swallowed a bite of salad, sat back and wiped his mouth with the linen napkin. Clearing his throat, he took a sip of wine. "Oh, same old thing. I have a new patient who is 90, has Alzheimer's and is as cantankerous as the day is long."

"Oh, that bad, eh?" Heather giggled.

Robert always could make her laugh. Well, she thought, always wasn't very long. In fact, a few days ago, she didn't even know he existed. Now, she could feel herself starting to crave his presence when he was away. His musky scent, the cute curl that always seemed to work its way from its place to fall on his freckled forehead, his warm, open smile with the tooth that was slightly crooked.

"What'd you ladies do today?"

"Not much." Heather answered. "You know what was odd though?"

"No, what?" Robert kept eating, barely listening.

"I was looking for Nikki earlier and found her in the attic. When I walked in, she was acting like she was hiding something."

Robert's fork stopped mid-way between his plate to his mouth. He placed his fork back on the plate and reached for his wine glass.

"Hiding what?"

"That's just it. I didn't get to find out. It seemed like she didn't even want to tell me. All I know is that it was some kind of book."

"Was it the diary that her uncle left? Did it say where the pink diamond is?" The words tumbled out of his mouth.

"Like I said, I really don't know."

"Well, why don't we get it and find out?"

Robert drew closer to Heather and she squirmed in her seat, backing up a few inches as he wrapped his strong hands around her wrist. Heather tried to break free to no avail. Robert tightened his grip and pulled her toward him.

"Robert. You're scaring me."

"Why don't we get it and find out?" He repeated through clenched teeth.

Robert stood, dragging Heather up with him, twisting her arm around her back.

"Ouch! Robert, you're hurting me!"

"I'll do a lot more than that if you don't get that diary!"

Heather felt the gun jam into her back. Her mind raced.

"Robert it's in a safe and I don't know the combination."

"Move!" Robert pushed Heather through the dining room door.

****

Greg snapped his fingers. "Oh, I forgot, Robert asked me to fill the tank up. We need to make a stop before I take you home. Is that okay?"

"Fine," Nikki said with more hostility than she felt, and she wished that she could take it back as soon as she said it. "Fine", she softened her tone.

They drove in silence to the only station in town. Greg paid for the gas, and reached across to the glove compartment, where Robert kept his book that he kept track of his milage. He opened it and a receipt fell out on the floor. Nikki picked it up.

"Greg, look at this!"

He looked at it and saw it was a receipt from The Stargazer for Pu-erh Tea.

"It can't be!" He grabbed it out of her hand. "I don't believe it! Not Robert. Anybody but him."

"But it's there in black and white, Greg. Robert has to have..." She stopped just short of declaring the unthinkable.

"Isn't he with Heather now?"

"Yes, I think he was to come for dinner about now." Nikki said anxiously.

Greg started up the hill as fast as he dared to in the weather. He skidded to a stop in front of the manor house. "You stay here!"

"Not on your life," Nikki answered as she swung the car door open. By the time she got up to the porch, Greg had already had his left hand on the icy handle, and his gun in his right .

****

Harry came out from his hiding place in the corner, and scooted up the servants stairs to the second floor landing. From there he spied Robert nudging Heather up the first flight of stairs.

"Move, Heather!"

"Robert, I don't know the combination."

"Then Nikki must. We'll just stay here and wait for her to come home. You had better hope that she values your friendship more than she does that diamond."

Harry slowly, stealthily came around to the Johnson family's solid wood linen cabinet that had been around for multiple generations. Because of his enormous size, Harry was certainly not going to risk being seen or heard, so used his powers to invisibly teleport himself to the top and crouched down to wait. He wasn't going to let Robert kill again.

****

Greg threw the door open and rushed in, with Nikki not far behind him. They both stopped dead in their tracks when they looked up on the second landing off the long staircase. There, beside her Great Great Grandma's cabinet, stood Robert and Heather. When Robert saw the two of them gawking at him, he grabbed Heather and held a gun to her head. Heather screamed.

"Shut up!" Robert growled at her.

"Now, Robert, you really don't want to do this." Greg said, slowly moving closer to the staircase.

"Either I get the jewel, or I kill her, take your pick."

Heather did her best to get away from him, but Robert had too tight of a hold on her.

Nikki started, "I don't have...".

Robert cut her off. "Oh, don't give me that. Tell me or end up like your aunt."

"It was you that poisoned her tea? You killed her? Why, Robert?"

"She wouldn't give me money that I needed to pay off all the loan sharks that were hounding me. I came to her asking...no...*pleading* with her, to sell the diamond and help me pay what I owe them. Do you think that she would? No." Mockingly now, he added, "She said that she didn't know if there even *was* a pink diamond, or where it was if it existed. I knew she was lying!"

He dragged Heather two steps back away from them, right under the antique cabinet. "Well, if you value your friend's life, you'll show me where it is. NOW!"

Greg shot his arm out to stop Nikki from going up the stairs. "No," she moaned.

In that moment, Harry jumped on Robert's head and clawed at his eyes. Blood from his forehead was trickling down his cheeks. As Robert reached up to protect his already bloodied face, he dropped the gun. Heather took that moment to run to the stairs going up to the third floor, but stopped when she heard Greg's voice.

"This is the hardest thing I have ever had to do." Greg said as he slipped his handcuffs over Robert's wrists and led him downstairs. "You have the right to remain silent, and by the way, I'd use it if I were you."

Chapter 21

Christmas Day

Nikki sat in the wingback armchair near the window. The purple velvet material encompassed her, making her feel comfortable and safe. The fire on the hearth warmed the otherwise drafty parlor. Looking out the bay window at the crisp morning, the blue sky was bright, as if last night never happened. But it did. She will always remember the terror she felt as Robert held her best friend at gunpoint.

Nikki took the diary from its hiding place between the cushions on the chair. She could hardly believe that Harry, her Harry, had been here since 1815. Franklin Johnson had written that Harry was a special cat and knew more than any other cat.

"Magic seems to happen wherever he is. He is a lucky charm to all who hold him dear. The Johnsons will always have this mystical cat that is as rare as a pink diamond."

Nikki heard Greg approaching and quickly placed the diary back in its hiding place.

When Greg came into the room, he sat quietly, gazing into the fire. After a few minutes, he finally broke the silence.

"How are you feeling today? I saw that Heather is still upset."

"Well, who can blame her? She finds out that the man she is falling in love with is a murderer? She is so lucky that we got to them in time. There is no telling what that crazy lunatic would have done to her."

Greg sat still. His head was bent low, like that of a guilty man. "I'm sorry, Nikki."

Nikki tore her eyes from the mesmerizing fire. "Why? You didn't do anything. You couldn't have known. Really, Greg, I don't want you blaming yourself. Anyway, things turned out for the best. Robert is locked up, where he belongs. He can't hurt anyone ever again. Heather is alright, a little shaken up, but alright."

Greg turned his gaze on her. "We never did find The Pink Diamond."

Nikki smiled knowingly at Harry, who was lying by the fire, purring loudly. She knew that she had a treasure more precious than any mineral. Harry and the wonders of his magic taught her that she had always had what was most important in life, the richness of love and friendship.

****

It was Christmas afternoon and Harry got the best present ever. Greg and company caught and put away Lynn's killer. None of the humans would have guessed that Robert had murdered her. Harry never did trust him. Something just didn't ring true about Robert Hayes. Come to find out, that wasn't even his real name. Miller was his name, and it turned out that his family and the Johnsons had some bad blood between them, all over the Pink Diamond. *All over me*, he thought smugly.

"Hey, Dewey! Get the gang together! We're having a party at The Fence!"

"Oh, boy! A cat party! Cool!" Dewey took off running as fast as he could.

Harry trotted down the sidewalk. It had snowed last night. The air was so cold that Harry could see his breath. The ice beneath his paws was frigid. Harry looked up in time to see the neighbor as he slipped. He tried to regain his balance, but to no avail. Down he went. Hard. Harry listened as a string of expletives poured from the man's mouth. Harry smiled to himself, shook his massive head and strolled on his way.

It had been a while since the gang had something good to celebrate...something really, really good! *This is clearly a good omen for the coming new year,* Harry thought.

When the whole gang came together, they all cheered Dewey, Ollie and most of all Little Bea, who came through when Harry needed her.

"Ahem. Quiet, please."

All the cats hushed up and Harry had the floor.

"I need to thank you all for doing your part to help bring justice for Lynn and Nikki. I especially want to acknowledge the three cats who made it all possible: Ollie, with your big heart, you were always ready to help; Dewey, you were fast and cunning; and last but certainly not least, Little Bea, you showed courage and tenacity. You got into places that all of us big cats couldn't possibly access. You three are awesome! Each and every one of you has been supportive, and I'm proud to know you all. This is a Merry Christmas indeed... now, let's party!"

The group of cats made a tight circle. Paws went in.

"Go, Cat Gang, go!

CPSIA information can be obtained
at www.ICGtesting.com
Printed in the USA
LVHW081950280419
615815LV00012BA/232/P